TWO PATHS
IN
THE WILDERNESS

by *Ellen Eaton Wilson*

*So nice to know
you!,
Ellen*

*Illustrations by
Richard Hultberg
Cover and maps
by J. Eve Griffin*

Published by CRANE

For Aunt Mary and Anna

" .....Your book TWO PATHS.., pulls together all the legends and stories the children have read so far. I read one or two chapters to the class each day. They were enthralled. The relationship between the two young men held the attention of both the boys and the girls. Because of our location, the students could imagine the action happening all around them. The children were fascinated with how the Indians obtained their names.

Your book really made that part of history come alive for them. ...thank you for sharing such a wonderful story with us."

Sincerely,
Arlene Goldstein
fourth grade teacher Barrington, RI

" ....I loved your book. My favorite part was when they met for the last time. My second favorite part was when they met for the 1st time......"

Megan Speed
Grade four Sowams School, Barrington, RI

INTRODUCTION

Long before 1492, when Christopher Columbus sailed to the "new world", a Native People lived and flourished. They left no written history; no chronicles, nor maps, but they did leave many other things. If you've walked in the fields and woods around your homes, you might have found a stone resting on a furrow, or nestled in the grass. Looking at it closely, you might have discovered an Indian arrow point, or scraper, or other stone tool. It might even have been a piece of broken pottery.

If you've discovered these long ago treasures, I'm sure it has invoked within you a wonder and curiosity of theses ancient peoples, who lived among the hills, fields, forests, and waterways long before the "Longknives" came.

We all learned about Columbus' voyage in 1492, the founding of St. Augustine, Florida in 1565,

Jamestown, Virginia in 1607 and Plimoth, Massachusetts in 1620, but what happened to the Native Americans who were already here when the Europeans claimed this land for themselves?

Perhaps we should look at and remember the contact period between the two worlds and the events that would forever change the cultures - both Native American and settlers in the "New World".

In the New England area, at one time, there were thousands of inhabitants belonging to many different tribes all speaking a form of the Algonquian language and moving in cycles and patterns of culture that had existed for thousands of years.

This story is about those Native Americans who lived in what we call "Southern New England," and what happened to them in 1675-1676 when their leader Metacom (whose English given name was King Philip) decided to rid his land of the invading *Awuanaguss* (Englishmen).

The events in this story are based on historical facts. Metacom (King Philip) was the second son of Massasoit, the Wampanoag Indian leader, who met the Plimoth Plantation settlers in 1621. Metacom became the leader of the Wampanoags in 1662, after his brother, Wamsutta (King Alexander), died. Metacom was forced to swear his loyalty to the English settlers and to promise to remain peaceful. By 1675, much of his Wampanoag tribal territory had been purchased by the Englishmen for blankets and hoes and strings of wampum, a form of money used at that time (made from shells of a large clam called a quahog). Metacom and his people were being squeezed, and animosity developed on both sides.

In the winter of 1675, Metacom's advisor, (Harvard educated, converted Christian, and Metacom's interpreter) John Sassamon, disappeared. His body was discovered that Spring and, according to the English, suspicion pointed to the Wampanoags. In the first part of June, in Plimoth, three Wampanoag Indians were tried for Sassamon's murder. They were found guilty. At the same time, Warriors were arriving in the Indian village of Mauntop (Mount Hope) joining Metacom's forces. Swanzey men from their nearby village were detained by some of these hostile Indians when they went to Metacom's land to claim some stray horses. Metacom intervened and insisted the settlers be released. He wanted no trouble until he was ready.

Soon after, the inevitable war erupted as actions by both Indians and settlers led to confrontations. Job Winslow's house in Swanzey was ransacked. Other Swanzey homes were attacked and burned. The war spread throughout the New England area.

The battles at The Great Swamp in the Narragansett winter village, battles in the Connecticut Valley of the Nipmuc territory during springtime, and the battle at Mount Hope on the Bristol peninsula in the summer of 1676, all took place.

It is my hope that through the eyes of Caleb, Will, Ontaquos and Tomaquog, the reader will think about those events so long ago that forever changed the peoples' lives and their destinies, and perhaps, by reading this story, will learn to "walk in each others' moccasins."

EW

TWO PATHS IN THE WILDERNESS

I
THE TRAPLINE

"Watch out for the Longknives!" Ottucke handed her son his robe.

"Why don't they like us?" Niccone settled the cloak around his shoulders. The deer hair tickled his neck and he scratched.

"They want our land, and Metacom says he'll give no more," said his mother.

"He's right. We need our land for hunting. I'm glad he's our leader and will protect us."

"May your traps be full, my son." Ottucke hugged him and turned back to the simmering pot in the firepit. She stirred it. "We could use some fresh meat."

Niccone grabbed his snowshoes, slung his quiver case over his shoulder, and took his bow. "I'm sure some of my traps caught something."

He walked down the main aisle of the longhouse. His friend, Whauksus, was rubbing bear grease and red powder on his body.

"This will keep me warm," he said lathering his arms and legs. Finished with the mixture, he grinned at Niccone. "I'll bring back more game than you will," he said.

"We'll see." Niccone continued down the long corridor and pushed aside the mat that covered the opening leading to the outside. He went through the outer door. Sun God's glare blinded him. He shielded his eyes until they adjusted.

After a long walk, he reached his first trap. Rabbit bones and fur littered the area. Wildcat tracks crisscrossed the crusty snow. Niccone checked each of his snares. The wildcat's footprints covered the snow around each one. Every trap held mutilated bits of animals or nothing.

"I'll get that wildcat," he muttered.

He followed the trail. It led to a steep rocky path high above an open plain. Niccone carefully examined the area. Finally, he crawled forward and stood in the clearing. He saw a small cave entrance. He cautiously approached the opening and found the cave empty. He looked skyward. Sun God hung pale and wan in the late winter afternoon. He nodded to Sun God, then slowly retraced his steps and followed his trail home.

Inside the longhouse he passed Whauksus. "Look. We eat well tonight." Whauksus held up a beaver. "What are you bringing back for your cookpot?" he asked grinning triumphantly.

"Nothing." Niccone smiled ruefully.

"I'm sure you'll do better when Sun God comes again," said his friend patting him on the shoulder. "It gets harder and harder with the Longknives turning our hunting lands into their farms."

Niccone nodded and walked toward his living compartment.

His mother looked up expectantly.

"I have nothing. A wildcat got all my traps. I'll go after him when Sun God sends his first rays."

"I know you'll succeed," said Ottucke.

II
THE BOBCAT'S LAIR

"Caleb, ye'd best call Lad. 'Twould appear a wildcat's dragged off one of our sheep." Tom took down his gun, powder horn, and bullet pouch.

"Be careful. If ye be in the Wilderness, watch for those Wampanoag heathens." Abigail handed her son his scarf and mittens.

"Why do they be such a problem?" asked Caleb.

Abigail said, "They take our hoes and cloth and wampum bead money for their lands and then keep hunting on them after we've bought them fair and square.

" 'Twas much better in the early years when we English dealt with Massasoit and we all lived in peace together. His son, Metacom, seems bent on trouble. If ye find yerself confronting one of his heathen, shoot him."

Tom winked at Caleb and handed him his gun. "Reason first. Most men would rather talk than fight."

Caleb smiled at Tom and nodded. He hung the powder horn across one shoulder and the bullet pouch across the other.

Tom whistled for Lad. "While ye be gone, I'll build a stronger pen for the sheep and a shelter near them for Lad. He can guard them tonight."

Caleb patted Abigail's shoulder. "Fear not, Mother. 'Twill not take me long to follow the trail." He closed the door quickly.

Abigail stirred the embers in the fireplace and added more wood, then stood at the tiny window watching Caleb and Lad cross the open fields and disappear into the woods beyond. Her gaze shifted to a gnarled and naked apple tree at the edge of the clearing. Three tiny grave markers stood beneath the winter limbs.

"He'll come to no harm." Tom rubbed her rigid back.

"God be willing, " she sighed. Her shoulders slumped in resignation. She turned to the hearth, piled coals on top of her Dutch oven lid, and prayed silently for her son's safety.

In the cold, raw, late afternoon, trudging along through the wilderness, Caleb slowly followed the tracks. After an hour, Lad sniffed, then bounded up an incline and disappeared. Caleb heard him barking in the distance and struggled up the steep slope. Reaching the clearing, he saw a cave. Lad stood barking outside. Caleb approached cautiously. He peered inside. It was empty.

"Come on, Lad," he said, turning for home. "We'll catch him on the morrow."

III
A FAIR TRADE

Niccone left the longhouse and slipped outside the huge palisade fence that surrounded the village. Sun God was pushing Moon Woman out of the sky. Niccone hurried along the trail and finally arrived at the wildcat's lair. Climbing the steep incline, he searched for signs of the cat. There were none. He settled into a crevasse at the edge of the clearing. The wind blew snow that covered his tracks. He waited.

Far away in the warm mainroom of his Swanzey farmhouse, Caleb pulled on his heavy boots, shrugged on his greatcoat, and grabbed his weapon. Abigail handed him a pouch filled with journey cakes, and he smiled at her. She started to say something, then sighed and turned toward the hearth. Caleb patted her shoulder, walked to the door, stepped outside and whistled for Lad, who was nowhere around. Caleb called several times, then trudged off once again to follow the wildcat's trail. He wished Lad had come with him.

After several hours, he reached the incline. Climbing the steep, snow covered, rocky trail, he finally arrived at the clearing. The snow had not been disturbed. He nestled in a hollow with his loaded gun and waited.

In the distance, a raucous crow cackled at an intruder's presence. Niccone watched fascinated as the lithe, sinewy wildcat padded silently into the clearing. His large paws splayed out, much like snowshoes, spreading his weight and keeping him from sinking into the snow. His lush thick coat, brown with underlying darker spots, outlined his powerful, but small muscular body. His lips, pulled slightly back, revealed fierce sharp teeth. Only his size surprised Niccone. He was the size of the dogs that lived in the Wampanoag village, and his tail was short as though someone had chopped part of it off. Niccone watched him sniff suspiciously then walk toward the cave.

Anxious to kill the destroyer of his food supply, Niccone aimed his arrow at the cat's chest and let it fly. At that instance, a deafening explosion filled the clearing. Niccone sucked his breath in and held it. He grabbed for a second arrow, and let his breath out slowly. His heart hammered against his chest. His eyes, darting wildly, probed everywhere as his ears strained to hear anything. What had he heard? Who had made it? Where had it come from? What should he do? Niccone stayed hidden, aiming his arrow at the clearing.

Across the way, Caleb strode toward the dead animal. He kicked it with his boot. He gasped when he saw the arrow. Where had it come from? And when? His fingers shook as he loaded his gun rapidly. He spun around, looking for anything moving. His heart tried to pound right through his rib cage. He sucked on his cheeks to clear his dry throat.

Then, Niccone rose silently from his hiding place, and slowly stepped toward Caleb, his arrow pointed at Caleb's chest. He looked into blue eyes for the very first time.

Caleb remembered what his father had said about talking rather than fighting, and held onto the thought as he watched the Indian cross the clearing, but he kept his finger on the trigger and scowled at the bow and arrow.

Niccone and Caleb meet

The two boys glared at one another.

Finally, Caleb cradled his musket and raised one hand. "Netop." He hoped his voice sounded firm.

Niccone frowned. Where had this *Awuanaguss* learned his word for 'friend'?

"Are ye alone?" Caleb looked all around.

Niccone looked puzzled.

"Me one." Caleb held up one finger.

"Nquit," Niccone answered holding one finger.

"Netop," Caleb repeated.

"Netop," answered Niccone, his face grave and unsmiling.

Caleb held his gun in one hand, grabbed the animal by the scruff of its neck, and pointed to the bullet hole.

Niccone lowered his bow still clutching its arrow at the bowstring and pointed to his arrow deeply imbedded in the rib cage. The two of them stared at each other.

Finally, Niccone put his arrow in his quiver case, slung his bow over his shoulder and took out his knife. Caleb aimed his gun at Niccone.

Niccone knelt, slipped the sharp point under the skin, and began skinning the hide.

Caleb watched for a minute, then rested his gun against a log, took out his knife and started skinning as well. When the hide was free, they dropped it next to the body.

Caleb held out his knife and reached for Niccone's at the same time. Niccone hesitated, then swapped weapons. Caleb liked the feel of the antler handle. He ran his finger along the stone blade. It cut him. He winced. Niccone grinned, then carefully ran his finger along Caleb's steel blade. It nicked him. The two boys laughed. Each one tried cutting a stick with the other's knife and was pleased with the way it worked.

Niccone put Caleb's knife next to the skinned carcass, pointed to it and then to himself. Caleb nodded, put the stone blade with the antler handle next to the soft, furry, hide, pointed to them, then to himself. Each boy nodded to the other, picked up his bundle and left the clearing. Just before they disappeared on their own paths in the wilderness, each turned.

"Netop," they called together, and laughed as they waved good bye to each other.

IV
THE STORM

The snow fell quietly and steadily, pricking Niccone's eyelids. He blinked frequently. It covered his head, his fur cloak, and the slimy body slung on his shoulder. Blood from the bobcat's wounds had caked and congealed into dark stains on its body which was stiffening and beginning to freeze. Niccone shifted it to his other shoulder.

He loped through the forest looking for his tribe's trailmark. He picked his way among the huge trees. He stopped, then smiled. Ahead of him, cut into a tall pine, he saw the mark.

Suddenly a branch crackled behind him. He spun around, dropping the cat. A huge figure hurtled out of the swirling snow and grabbed him. Niccone tried desperately to escape. His heart speeded and he fought fiercely, kicking at the strong legs that backed against his. He felt himself lifted into the air and slammed onto the frozen ground. His head ached. His vision blurred. His assailant straddled his chest, pinning his arms into the snow.

His eyes cleared, and he stared into his father's face.

Kuttiomp released his grip, stood up, and hauled Niccone to his feet. "What did you learn just now?" he asked, brushing the snow from his son's cloak.

Niccone trembled with relief. "Well," he answered, "If I'd been more alert, I'd have seen you slip behind me and been ready for your attack."

"Good. You must learn to anticipate your enemy's moves. Come, the storm gets worse. Let's go home."

Niccone retrieved his wildcat and followed his father. In single file, the two of them hurried through the white clouds of swirling snow.

Nunummatin, the North wind, howled and caught their words, swallowing them in his own frenzied screech. Snow forced their eyelids shut and they blinked to clear them. They trudged on. Finally the palisade surrounding the village loomed ahead. They found its narrow entrance and followed the path to their own longhouse. Stumbling into the outer entrance with rasping coughs of relief, they waited to catch their breath. Adjusting to the gloom, they entered the main room. Niccone inhaled the familiar smells of bear grease, curing hides, bubbling stew pots, and thick, hazy blue smoke. It smelled good.

Along the central corridor, children shouted chasing each other in a game of tag. Niccone laughed, watching Shannuke's small brown body skillfully avoid the cooking pots slung over the firepits in the aisle. His brother's name, Little Squirrel, suited him.

Niccone turned to his father. "He didn't see us. Next time maybe he'll be more alert."

"Like someone else I know." His father looked at him.

He nodded ruefully.

Passing family compartments, they arrived in their own section in the middle of the enormous dwelling. Niccone dropped the stiff body in the shadows near their sleeping bench. Ottucke looked up to see who cast the shadow on her firepit. With a cry of delight, she rushed to embrace Kuttiomp who emerged from the smoky haze. "I'm so glad you're home. It has been so lonely without you."

"It's good to be back." Kuttiomp stroked her cheek, smiling down at her.

Ottuke took his cloak and put the bearskin next to the fire. She took Niccone's deerskin cloak, hanging it next to his father's. "I was worried when the storm started. I'm so glad you're safe."

Niccone smiled at her.

"You both must be hungry. Sit. I'll feed you."

They collapsed wearily on the edge of the sleeping platform. She reached under the wide bench and took out two wooden bowls, filling them from the cookpot. They ate hungrily. Finally they finished and sat back. Kuttiomp wiped his hand across his mouth, rubbed his stomach, and reached for his tobacco pouch. "How have things gone since I've been away?"

"I've missed you, but we've been all right. Niccone's traps are not always full but we have enough." Ottucke wiped their bowls with a small piece of soft deerhide and pushed them back under the bench.

"Wait 'til I tell you what happened today..." Niccone began.

"You must wait to be spoken to." Kuttiomp's voice was stern.

Niccone edged his way into the shadows away from the hearth. His mother raised an eyebrow and smiled ever so slightly at him. He sighed, waiting for his father to continue, but Kuttiomp had stopped speaking and rose to greet a figure coming down the aisle toward them.

V
TALK OF TROUBLE

Niccone sat on the sleeping platform. His grandfather, Pequawas, shuffled along the aisle, stepped around the firepit, and stood silently in the firelight facing Kuttiomp. Kuttiomp licked his own forearm in the traditional greeting of the Wampanoags.

Pequawas raised a thin wrinkled arm and licked it. "I just heard you were back." He settled next to Niccone, on the soft furs He patted Niccone's leg and smiled at him.

Ottucke lit a twig and ignited a torch over the bed. Its light flickered on Pequawas' face deepening his wrinkles. Niccone thought, "He's well named. He looks like a 'Grey Fox' with his grey hair, sharp features and wise eyes." He smiled at his grandfather.

His father spoke. "I've come on ahead of the hunting party." Kuttiomp offered Pequawas tobacco. "We found Longknives in our hunting territory. They seem to be everywhere."

"I met one today," interrupted Niccone. He waited to see if he could speak.

"Tell us what happened," Kuttiomp commanded, nodding his head for Niccone to continue.

Niccone smiled at his father and began. "I met a young Awuanaguss today when I was hunting." He told them of his encounter.

"You did well," said Kuttiomp. "But there could have been trouble. Not all Awuanaguss treat us like this one."

"I remember when the Longknives first came," said Pequawas. "I was the age of Niccone. Metacom's father pledged our people to be friends and allies, and our two peoples have kept the treaty for more moons than I can count. I'm certain Metacom can settle our differences as his father did so many moons ago."

"I'm not so sure," said Kuttiomp. "When the treaty was made, there were only a few Awuanaguss settled in the small town they call Plimoth. Now there are as many Longknives as the pigeons that blot out the sun when they fly to our cornfields. The Longknives build their towns and hunt our game and cut down our forests."

"Do you think there will be trouble?" asked Ottucke.

"It's possible," said Kuttiomp.

"We must continue to live together," said Pequawas.

"It may be too late," answered Kuttiomp.

"The Longknife today..." Niccone looked to see if Kuttiomp would object.

Kuttiomp nodded his approval.

"He and I worked things out even though we couldn't speak each others' words."

"Not all Awuanaguss are Netops," warned Kuttiomp. "I will see Metacom. He and the Council will decide what is best. Now don't you want to give your mother something?" Kuttiomp smiled at Niccone.

Niccone slid off the furs and dragged the carcass over to his mother.

"We'll eat well while this storm rages." She hugged him, then began butchering the animal, dropping chunks of meat into the boiling cookpot. She smiled at Niccone. "You're tired. Here's your dry robe. Crawl into bed and sleep well. You're a fine hunter and a fine son." She covered him with his warm cloak. The furs tickled his cheek but felt good against his naked body.

Pequawas patted his shoulder. "You did well today."

Niccone nodded sleepily, burrowing into the piles of furs. "I wish all Awuanaguss were like the one I met today," he said.

"So do I," replied Pequawas sighing.

VI
CALEB'S STORY

Lad rose from the hearth, went to the door, and pawed at it quietly, turning his head toward Abigail who was busy shifting cooking pots in the huge hearth. He whined.

"Lie down, Lad," Abigail commanded, pointing to his straw bed.

Lad turned, slinking back to his place near the fire. He twirled himself around three times, then grunted as he reluctantly settled down, his baleful eye riveted on the door. He raised his head and sniffed the air, thumping his tail in spite of Abigail's stern scowl.

Abigail left the hearth and peered out through the tiny window into the bleak snowy late afternoon gloom. Swirling snow and the impenetrable forest loomed undisturbed in the dusk. Abigail studied the scene, searching for Caleb, then turned disconsolately back to the hearth. She reached for a small lamp near the fireplace and, filling it with oil, trimmed and floated its tiny wick. Inserting a thin twig into the fireplace, she lit the wick and hung the lamp in the window. Its small sputtering flame dispersed the evening gloom around it and flickered its message of welcome to the darkness beyond.

Tom entered, kicking snow from his boots and shaking his greatcoat before hanging it on its hook. Lad leaped up to greet him. Tom scrubbed the dog's ears. "Lie down, Lad," he said dropping into his chair wearily.

Outside, Caleb emerged into the open fields. He squinted, searching for a familiar landmark. The tiny lamp glow lead him on. Entering the farmyard, he groped at the corn crib and stuffed the hide onto a shelf under the crib roof. No sheep would smell it there.

Reaching the house, he stomped his heavy boots on the snow-covered granite slab outside, lifted the latch, and hurried inside. Lad bounded from his bed, swung his tail in an erratic circle of ecstasy, and barked, nudging his muzzle under Caleb's hand. Caleb stooped, patting the broad head, then ruffled Lad's thick winter coat.

"Praise be yer home." Abigail hurried toward Caleb, taking his coat and hanging it near the hearth along with his hat, mittens, and scarf. She turned to tend the kettles and pots nestled in the coals, and rushed to serve supper.

Tom looked up from the table where he'd settled. "Did ye find the creature?"

"Aye." answered Caleb, "His hide's in the corn crib." He removed his boots and set them on the edge of the hearth. Caleb replaced the musket on the wall and hung up the powderhorn and bullet pouch, then joined Tom.

"And the carcass?"

"I shared it with a Wampanoag. I got the hide and traded for his stone knife. He got my knife."

"Wampanoag." Abigail had spun from the hearth at the word. "Ye could have been killed. I warned ye about the Wilderness." She shook her ladle for emphasis.

"Now, woman, let's hear the lad's story."

Caleb told them what happened between mouthfuls of hot cornbread lathered with butter. " 'Twas hard dealing with the Wampanoag, not knowing his language," said Caleb.

Abigail filled their plates, slopping chicken stew with a hurried motion of anger, then sat down, her back rigid in disapproval.

"Did ye cross into Indian lands?" asked Tom.

"No. I walked west 'til I came to the rocky hills. I'm sure 'tis part of our Charter lands from Plimoth."

"Good. We don't want trouble with King Philip and his tribe. Ye did right with the Indian." Tom sopped his gravy with a hunk of bread. " 'Twas only right to split the spoils. And I'd say yer trade was good. The Indian sounds like an honest enough soul."

"Honest, maybe," said Abigail, "but he's a heathen nonetheless.

"Now, goodwife, ye know as well as I that there's good and bad in every lot."

" 'Tis true," admitted Abigail. "But it just bothers me to think of Caleb alone in the wilderness with the heathens."

Tom rose and went to her. "I know ye fear for your only young'un," he said, tenderly patting her shoulder, "but the lad's well taught and nearly grown."

Their voices droned on. Caleb sat with his elbows on the table, propping his head with both hands. He closed his eyes.

"Caleb, ye'd best go to bed."

Caleb looked sleepily at his mother. He yawned, nodded, stretched and stood up. He went to the cupboard and took down a lamp, "Good night," he said, scratching Lad and turning toward the loft.

He climbed the stairs and crawled toward his mattress. He blew out the light and dove under the covers, pulling the blankets up over his head. He wondered if the Indian had gotten home safely.

VII
EMPTY TRAPS

The silence woke him. The storm was over. Niccone crawled out of his warm bed, shivering in the predawn cold. He stretched, then bent to fix the fire. He blew gently. Small coals glowed red. He added more wood. Smoke twisted lazily toward the smokehole high above the firepit. Finally flames blinked, chasing shadows onto wall mats and dancing them across the sleeping figures still huddled under the warm furs.

Sun God sent a soft grey color through the open smokehole of the domed bark roof. Niccone dressed. In the early morning light, he exchanged smiles with his mother, who'd awakened. She slipped from the sleeping platform, stood and pulled her deerskin dress over her head. She scooped stew from the steaming kettle hung over the fire he'd built, and handed him his bowl.

He tasted wildcat. It was good. Niccone finished eating. Grabbing his food pouch and weapons, he reached under the bench once more and dragged out his snowshoes.

"Let's hope my traps are full," he said to his mother, throwing his robe over his shoulder.

Ottucke smiled at him then frowned. "With no Longknives to bother you."

"Don't worry. The Awuanaguss don't come where my snares are set." He patted her shoulder gently and left.

Stepping into Sun God's blinding glare, he waited for his eyes to adjust. Shannuke and his friends played in the deep snow drifts. Their naked bodies, covered with animal fat, flashed in the sunlight. He remembered stinging toes and fingers turned red from the cold and snow that drove him and his friends in to the warmth and the comfort of the longhouse when he was little.

Leaving the children behind, he slipped between the village's high fences' narrow opening, put on his snowshoes, and headed for his line of traps.

Working his way through the drifts, he reached the first trap. He looked down in disgust. "Wolves. How I hate them!" He peeled a fleshless carcass from his willow snare and threw it in the snow. He baited the trap and trudged on to the next one. It was empty. As Sun God traveled across the sky, Niccone wound his way carefully along the whole line of traps. Most were empty. Those that weren't empty, had only small, badly mutilated pieces of animal left by wolves.

Wearily he scanned the sky. Sun God was nearing his path to the underworld. Niccone started for home. He shuddered at the thought of being caught by Hobomok and the other night spirits.

29

VIII
CELEBRATION

Approaching his winter village, he heard excited cries and happy singing. Snowshoeing across the open area, he rushed through the entrance. Toboggans lay stacked with deer, moose, and a bear. He grinned with excitement. The great feast and winter festival would begin. He ran to find his friends.

They were gathered around the hunting party. He joined them and they all stood enthralled by stories the men told. Only the continual complaints about Longknives in the hunting territory marred the festive atmosphere.

Women and girls gathered carcasses and began skinning and butchering. Ottucke motioned to Niccone. "The men are hungry. We'll need much wood for our cooking. Go bring as much as you can find."

Niccone plodded toward the palisade opening, grumbling to himself. "When I'm a warrior, it'll be Shannuke who has to go, and I'll be telling stories of my hunting."

"Those who talk to themselves when no one is around are sometimes called possessed by Hobomok," a voice called behind him.

Niccone looked back quickly and laughed. His friend, Whauksus, hurried along on his snowshoes, racing to catch up.

"Wait up. You're not the only one out here for wood."

Niccone stopped. "I know, but, Whauksus, I can't wait to be a warrior and be standing telling of my adventures."

"I'm anxious too. All our age group is. Come on the quicker we get the wood, the sooner we'll be back to enjoy the festival."

Sun god left the sky. Only his afterglow lighted their way. Loaded down, they re-entered the village and dropped the wood at the cooking fires. Niccone smelled the meat sizzling, its fat dripping onto red-hot coals, then bursting into tiny clouds of blue smoke. He could taste every succulent morsel. His tongue ringed the inside of his mouth, and his thoughts focused on the tantalizing food.

Ottucke looked up through the heat and smoke. She nodded at him. "That's fine. Go join your friends."

Niccone found them in the Ceremonial

Lodge. He pushed his way in and stood next to Whauksus, who nudged him and pointed. "Look, your father's winning."

Kuttiomp knelt on a mat, deftly flashing brightly painted peach pits from under one moccasin to another. Whenever he stopped, warriors bet whether Kuttiomp's opponent kneeling opposite him could choose the moccasin hiding the peach pit. Niccone, Whauksus, and their friends laughed and watched each competitor try to outguess Kuttiomp. He defeated everyone, finally handing the pits to another man. Everyone cheered. Niccone grinned at his father who smiled back.

Niccone helped his mother carry huge platters of roasted meats, steaming pots of boiled acorns and cooked dried vegetables, and trays of corncakes sweetened with maple sugar. They brought the food to the Warriors all gathered in the Ceremonial Lodge.

Niccone stood impatiently with his friends watching the women feed the men first. Suddenly, Shannuke darted from the group of younger children and snatched a piece of meat from his father's bowl.

Everyone laughed when the little boy dropped it and rushed outside to plunge his burned hand into the soothing snow. Niccone followed Shannuke into the night to console him. When the two brothers returned, the women and younger children were busily dipping into mounds of food left by the warriors. The two boys joined in.

IX
DISCOVERED

Three times Sun God came, and the festival continued. Niccone's stomach bulged and ached from being so full. He left the warmth of the feasting lodge and went to look for Whauksus. Outside, long shadows stretched across the snow-covered clearing. The two friends stood quietly watching Sun God leave.

Niccone nudged Whauksus. "Look! The Warriors are gathering at the Council House. I wonder why. Let's go find out."

"Wait, we're never supposed to go near the Warriors. Only those who have passed the Warrior's test can enter," Whauksus said.

"What a great test for us to get close and not be discovered." Niccone was already slithering along the ground, keeping himself hidden in the darkening shadows as he crawled silently toward the lodge. He hissed at Whauksus, "Are you coming?"

Whauksus hesitated, then followed Niccone. Outside the front entrance outlined by a flickering firepit, two guards stood chatting. One turned his head in their direction. Niccone and Whauksus froze, blending into the darkness. The guard turned back to his companion. The boys continued. Finally, they huddled at the far corner of the structure, hiding in the deep shadows away from the entrance fire.

Scarcely breathing, they nudged one another as each warrior arrived. They watched Kuttiomp slip inside. A few minutes later, Whauksus' father appeared and pushed through the mat doorway. Others followed.

Moonwoman held her light at the edge of the earth. The two boys waited. It was very quiet inside the lodge. Slowly Moonwoman pushed her light into the night sky, dimming her brilliant stars and spreading a bright glow onto the snow.

Niccone and Whauksus heard snowshoes swishing along the winter path. They watched a figure approach the guards. The two warriors licked their arms and waited. The tall, muscular man with a strong, handsome face nodded and licked his arm in return. A bright red robe covered his shoulders. The boys glimpsed an embroidered English shirt beneath it. The two guards stepped respectfully aside.

"It's Metacom," they mouthed silently to each other. They watched him push the entrance mat out of the way.

The two friends crawled deeper into the shadows.

Metacom stepped inside. There was a growl of approval and welcome from the Warriors within. Voices raised in song and chanting as the Medicine Man invoked the spirits to protect and defend them and to guide them to wisdom and power. The boys waited, lying silently against the bark covering trying to hear. The voices were low.

They heard Metacom speak, "I've complained about encroachment many times. It does no good. If there's more trouble with the Longknives, we'll prepare all our young men for the Warrior Society."

The boys poked each other excitedly.

Metacom continued. "I'm beginning to think the only solution for us is to unite all the tribes, the Nipmucs, the Narragansetts, the Pequots and even the volatile Mohawks. We must plan carefully and be well prepared, but the only way to get our lands back is to drive the Awuanaguss into the sea."

Niccone and Whauksus looked at each other. As the discussion continued, the two friends crept away. On hands and knees with heads down, they silently crawled along the edge of the building. Suddenly Niccone bumped into a solid knee. Whauksus banged into him. They looked up. Staring down at them were the stern faces of the Warrior guards. Strong arms hauled them to their feet, propelling them toward the firelight.

Metacom and the others burst outside. "What is the disturbance?" asked Metacom.

The guards shoved Niccone and Whauksus forward. They stood, heads lowered, waiting.

"What are you boys doing here? You know no one but Warriors are allowed near the Council House," said Metacom.

Niccone nodded and raised his head to look into Metacom's eyes. So did Whauksus. Over Metacom's shoulder each boy saw his father standing, watching.

"Explain your presence," demanded Metacom, glowering at the two boys.

Niccone wondered if his voice would

work. His stomach churned. He thought he might be sick. He swallowed forcing his food to stay in his stomach. Finally, he stammered, "We are both of an age to be tested. I..I..I thought that if we could show our stealth and cunning, you would choose us to start on the path of the Warrior. We are anxious and ready to serve you."

Metacom waited. He looked at the boys and then towards his Council members. They stood stoically, each face bland and immobile. Neither Niccone nor Whauksus dared look at each other or at their fathers.

Then Metacom laughed. I accept your reasoning," he said. "But if you are going to be my Warriors, you both must learn to be more careful. A captive Warrior is a useless one."

"We realize that," said Niccone boldly, relieved at Metacom's response. "That is why we are anxious to train and be tested. There is much we must learn."

Metacom asked, "Who is your father?"

"Kuttiomp," said Niccone, looking at his father proudly.

"You reason like him. That is good." Metacom turned to Whauksus. "And you?"

he asked.

"I'm a good follower," stammered Whauksus.

All the Warriors laughed.

"You are important too," said Metacom, smiling. Then he looked serious. "You will soon be tested. But go to your longhouse now. There is much to be discussed here tonight and it is for Warriors only to decide."

Niccone and Whauksus turned and ran for home.

X
QUIET TALK

They stopped outside their longhouse. Niccone shook his friend's shoulder excitedly, "We'll start our Warrior journey soon."

Whauksus nodded, clapping Niccone on his back. He danced around him. "You're right. At last. Just think, we'll be Warriors with Warrior names."

The two boys imitating a yapping fox and a raucous crow, chased each other through the compound, finally collapsing in the entrance to the Longhouse.

"It was clever of you to think of that answer," said Whauksus.

"I had to think of something. Did you see my father watching?"

"Yes. At first I thought he'd be angry, but he looked quite proud when you'd finished." said Whauksus.

"Your right," agreed Niccone. "I was really scared."

"Me too," said Whauksus.

The two boys rested their heads against a wooden water barrel. "I wonder what our

Warrior names will be? You won't be Whauksus, the Red Fox, any more." said Niccone.

"Nor you, Niccone, the Black Crow," said Whauksus.

The two boys sat quietly staring up at the cured hides stored in the overhead storage space. Finally Niccone said, "Let's go home."

The two of them stepped silently through the inner doorway, pushed the mat aside, and went into the longhouse.

Later, Niccone sat pensively on his sleeping platform.

"What is it?" Ottucke asked.

Niccone told her what had happened.

She looked thoughtfully at her son. "You are fortunate Metacom found it amusing. You could have been severely punished."

"I know." Niccone had seen boys made to run the gauntlet. Some had taken many moons to heal. Niccone crawled under the warm furs. "I can't wait to be a warrior," he said.

His mother looked at him and patted his shoulder. "You'll be one soon enough," she sighed.

XI
MORNING CHORES

The winter wind whistled around the eaves, blew through the cracks and brushed across his face. Caleb pulled his head under his warm heavy blankets and scrunched into a smaller ball. His cornhusk mattress rustled against his shifting weight. A voice kept disturbing his dream. He scowled in his sleep.

"Caleb." His mother shook his shoulder. "Waken immediately."

Caleb opened his eyes and focused on Abigail's stern face. Only her head and shoulders appeared above the loft flooring. Caleb sleepily stared at her.

She leaned forward and shook him again. "How anyone can sleep as sound as ye, I just don't know. I've been calling ye since before dawn. Ye'll be late for school and Reverend Myles'll take a stick to ye."

She softened her frown and rumpled his thick blonde hair. "Hurry. I'll have yer breakfast ready for ye." She disappeared down the stairs.

The early morning cold bit at him as he crawled out from under the blankets. He rushed from the loft and skittered down to the main room hearth. Sunlight shone through the diamond-shaped window panes, making patterns on the broad pine floor.

Caleb took his wooden bowl from the cupboard and held it out. His mother filled it. He cupped his hands around it and sat eating on a small stool near the fire.

"Tell yer father his food be ready when he finishes in the barn."

"Aye." He put the bowl down and pulled on his boots, struggled into his coat, and jammed his hat on, wrapping his scarf around his neck.

"Don't tarry after lessons." She handed him his lunch pail.

He smiled at her, but she'd already turned back to the hearth.

Outside, the frigid cold engulfed him. He pulled his scarf around his mouth, breathing in his own warmth. He followed his father's snowy footsteps to the barn. Inside, the glow from Tom's lamp led Caleb to his father.

"Ye be late. Ye'd best be quick with yer chores." Tom said, as he stored his pitchfork on a hook on the wall, handed Caleb the lamp and went to the barn door. Before stepping into the trampled snowy path, he spoke again, "The Guernsey's the only one left. When ye've finished cleaning her stall and bedding down the rest of the animals with fresh straw, ye may leave. Don't be late for school."

Caleb grabbed the pitchfork and hurried toward the cows. "I'll hurry. Mother said yer breakfast be ready."

"Aye." Tom stepped outside and closed the barn door against the bitter winter cold.

Caleb hurried through his chores, then saddled Blackie. He blew out the lamp. Leading the horse outside, he mounted quickly and rode hurriedly out of the barnyard. Lad came bounding toward him, barking and wagging his tail.

"Stay, Lad." The dog drooped and turned, slinking dejectedly back toward the farm. Caleb guided Blackie along the path. Leaving the open space of the fallow, snow-covered fields, he plunged into the forest. He shivered. The wind clacked top limbs of bare branches. They sounded like convicts' skeletons he'd seen hanging on the main road into Plimoth. He shuddered and urged Blackie on.

A few minutes later, he stopped at Will's farm. It felt good to be out of the woods. He hollered again for Will. Blackie stomped impatiently. Caleb waited.

Will came galloping out of his yard on his horse, his coat unbuttoned, his scarf flapping behind him. His hat perched precariously on his dark disheveled hair somehow managed to stay on his head. He urged his horse onto the trail and pulled up abruptly when he reached Caleb.

Breathlessly he began, "I thought ye'd gone without me."

Caleb laughed. "When the storm started yesterday, I figured ye'd be late."

Will buttoned his coat, straightened his hat, and tied his scarf. "Ye'd be right."

XII
LATE FOR SCHOOL

The two friends soon plunged back into the forest. Caleb felt better with Will galloping behind him.

"Did ye ever notice how dark it gets in the woods?" Will shouted.

Caleb turned back and yelled, "Aye, 'tis better when we come to farms and rivers."

Will reined up behind Caleb, who went first over a small wooden bridge. "Woods is Indian country, that's what 'tis."

"Aye," Caleb answered. "And they surely manage it the way they hunt and fish and move around planting their crops and all."

"There be something scary about the way they slip in and out so quiet," Will said. "Ye can't trust them."

"Maybe," said Caleb, "but remember without the Wampanoags, the Plimoth settlers would've starved their first winter, and the Wampanoag I told ye about was certainly fair when we divided up the wildcat we'd both shot."

"Well, I don't trust the Wampanoags."

"Have ye met or dealt with one?"

"Well, no..."

"Let's not argue. We're late enough as 'tis." Caleb bent forward, kicked Blackie's sides, and galloped ahead with Will following close behind.

Passing scattered farms, they approached a wide, fast-moving river. Stubble of marsh grass pushed through the snow along the banks. On either side, marshland spread into open flat areas clotted with frozen patches of ice and snow. A bridge spanned the river, stretching on to a road that led to the center of Swanzey. The trail skirted the long snow-covered fence marking the start of Wampanoag land to the east.

Myles' garrison loomed massive against the sky, the last house before the bridge.

The two friends galloped to the lean-to behind the house, slid from their mounts, pushed through the horses already tethered, and tied their reins to the hitching post. They adjusted feedbags and blankets, and grabbing their lunch buckets, hurried inside. Students were reciting their catechism. Reverend Myles sat at his desk near the huge fireplace. Caleb and Will saw him rise, his broad stocky figure outlining his clerical robe.

Standing before them in a shaft of smoky sunlight, he scowled. His flat cheeks glowed ruddy in the brisk temperature. His hazel eyes under thick eyebrows rose quizzically. "Ye be late."

Caleb and Will nodded. The other students stared waiting to see what would happen.

Frowning, Reverend Myles tapped his cane against the palm of his right hand. "Tardiness be a sin," he continued.

Caleb and Will remained silent. Each took a deep breath.

Reverend Myles tapped his cane once again. "The Lord punishes transgressors."

Daniel Leonard smirked. Will glowered at him. Caleb rubbed his hands along the side of his coat.

"However, since the Lord sent the storm and ye both live so far away, ye be excused this time. Take yer seats."

Will smiled triumphantly at Daniel. The two boys hung their coats up quickly and scrambled into their places on the bench in the back of the schoolroom.

48

"That was close," whispered Caleb.
"Aye, I'll be on time on the morrow," Will promised in a whisper.

XIII
STRANGER ON THE TRAIL

After school, Caleb and Will mounted their horses. The animals were anxious to be off. Winter winds had blown the snow and rearranged the drifts. A mile from the garrison, they stopped to rest the horses. Suddenly out of the woods, a tall, gaunt Indian came stumbling and weaving toward them.

"Look at that drunken sot of an Indian. 'Tis disgusting," Will yelled at Caleb. They guided their horses to the edge of the trail to avoid the wobbling figure and watched him hurtle forward, collapsing in the snow.

Caleb noticed blood. "Look, Will, he's not drunk. There's a gash on his head."

The two boys dismounted. The Indian moaned. They stared into his swarthy face with its high cheekbones and hawk nose. Blood caked his eyes. Caleb bent over him shaking, him gently. The Indian groaned again.

"Let's leave him." Will turned away, remounted, and started along the path.

"We can't. Remember what we learned in our Bible lesson. He's a human being in trouble. We can't leave him. Come on, Will, give me a hand."

"Do it yerself. I'm going home. Ye'd better come too." Will tugged on his reins and kicked his horse.

"I can't leave him. Come on, Will, help me get him to Reverend Myles."

"No."

Caleb glowered at his friend's retreating figure. He collected branches and vines and built a sled, then piled on fir boughs. The Indian moaned again as Caleb rolled him onto the sled. He covered him with Blackie's blanket, attached a long, strong vine to the front of the litter, and hooked the other end to his saddle. Blackie slowly dragged the man along the path back to Reverend Myles' garrison.

Once there, Caleb pounded on the door and hollered, "I've got a wounded Indian. Please help."

Mrs. Myles stuck her head out of an upstairs window. "Good heavens, what's all the commotion?"

"Please help." Caleb watched her startled face disappear and moments later, Reverend Myles opened the door and dashed outside. Caleb helped him carry the Indian inside.

Mrs. Myles waited near the hearth in the main room. She hastily dipped a cloth into her water bucket and began to gently remove the dried frozen blood from the Indian's forehead and around his eyes. Her short stocky body hovered over the wounded man. Her pudgy hands worked gently but firmly. A few minutes later, she spoke to her husband. "This wound needs stitching. I'll fetch my medicine bag."

The Indian opened his eyes. He stared at his two rescuers, then tried to lift his head. Blood spurted from the gash in his scalp and ran into his eyes again.

Just then Mrs. Myles returned. "Oh dear," she said. "Please don't move until I've sewn the wound." She cleaned the blood once again.

He gazed at her with soft, brown eyes. "I shall remain immobile," he answered in a low, weakened voice.

Caleb gasped. "Where did ye learn English?"

"At Harvard College."

Reverend Myles spoke. "Ye must be Sassamon, King Philip's interpreter."

"Aye. 'Tis so," he replied.

Mrs. Myles threaded her needle and began stitching the jagged edges of the wound together. Sassamon made no sound.

While his wife continued to work, the minister patted Caleb's shoulder. "Ye've done a good job. We'll see that he rests, and I'll talk with him later. Ye must get along home now before 'tis too dark."

Caleb nodded. He looked out the window at the waning sun and headed for the front door, tugging on his coat as he went.

"Good bye, Caleb. God go with ye," called Reverend Myles as Caleb closed the door behind him.

Mounting Blackie, he turned him toward the trail, once again urging him on.

Later, he rode into his farmyard. Lad bounded across the snowy fields to greet him and waited for him to dismount, then leapt up and licked Caleb's face. Caleb grabbed him playfully by the scruff and the two of them wrestled. Caleb watered, fed, and bedded Blackie down, and hurried to the house. Lad romped at his side. They entered just as the sun dropped below the horizon, its afterglow searing the sky with brilliant reds and golds.

Abigail glanced up quickly. "Thank the Lord ye be home." Her voice changed and she said sharply, "Where have ye been?"

He hung his coat on its peg and began to tell her. Tom returned from the sheep pen, pushing the door roughly and slamming it quickly. "Ye be late. Did ye have trouble?"

"No, but let me tell ye both what happened on the Swanzey Trail." His parents listened intently.

Caleb asked, "What do ye suppose the Indian was doing on the way to our village?"

The flickering lamp light emphasized Tom's scowl. Abigail stood waiting.

"These be uneasy times," Tom said. "There be rumors of meetings and Indian messengers traveling on our paths to get from one Indian camp to the next. It may be they be discussing the winter hunting, but it could also mean they are forming some kind of alliance with one another. King Philip, now

deep in his winter village would be their
natural leader."

Abigail brought steaming plates of lamb
stew to the table.

"I'll go into town tomorrow and find out
what's happening," Tom said as he picked up
his spoon.

"Well, if any young warriors prowl around
my home," announced Abigail, "I'll take a gun
to them. We've worked too hard and long to
make this a decent farm. I have no intention
of giving it up." She set mugs of hot cider
before them.

"Let's not make any more of it than 'tis,
cautioned Tom. He turned to his son. "Ye've
done a good thing helping a fellow human
being. I be proud of ye."

Caleb flushed.

" 'Twas a heathen," Abigail said.

Tom corrected her, " 'Twas a Christian
Indian."

" 'Twas a heathen nonetheless," Abigail
muttered, clearing away the plates.

Before Tom could answer, she said, " 'Tis
time for us to settle down for the night."
Abigail finished clearing the table and
banked the fire. She handed Caleb a lamp to

light his way to the loft, and then began to draw back the curtain that enclosed her and Tom's bed in the main room.

Caleb crawled up the narrow stairs to his mattress.

XIV
TOWN MEETING

The next morning, Caleb followed his father along the trail. A blinding sun had melted the drifts and turned the crusty frozen ice to slush in the January thaw. Arriving at the garrison, they dismounted and tied their horses to the hitching post. Inside, Tom joined neighbors seated at the benches normally used by the students. Caleb stood with his classmates along the outside edge of the room.

" 'Twould appear there be no school today," Will greeted Caleb.

Caleb scowled at Will. " 'Tis a good thing. I never did get my lessons done."

" 'Tis what happens when ye spend yer time helping ungrateful heathens," hissed Will.

"Hush." Caleb, flushed with anger, turned and focused on Reverend Myles who stood in front of the group. He raised his hand. "Yesterday," Reverend Myles began, "Caleb Eaton found an injured Indian on the Swanzey Trail not far from my house. He brought him here, and we ministered to him.

It was Sassamon, King Philip's interpreter. He recovered rapidly, and after rest and nourishment, he and I had a long talk.

"He left this morning. Before he went, he told me King Philip is upset with the expansion that's been taking place here in the wilderness. He said that King Philip claims the winter hunting is poor and that our animals have driven the forest animals away with their foraging."

"We've a right to turn our animals loose on our own property," said Will's father.

"We've bought our land fair," interrupted Job Winslow, who lived in the other end of town. "We paid what the Indians asked, and Philip himself signed the deeds."

"Aye," echoed some of the other Swanzey men.

" 'Tis true," Caleb's father stood facing his neighbors. "But they be getting squeezed. Look how small their territory's become. Once it was not only their summer village at Mauntop, but all of Swanzey and Rehoboth as well."

"Well, what are ye going to do about it now, Tom?" asked Will's father.

Tom answered, "What we need to do is to

make sure that ill feelings are carried no further. We must learn to live together and respect each other's ways. Otherwise, there could be bloodshed. And if an uprising happens when the Wampanoags are in their summer village, we'll be the first to be attacked."

Before anyone could say anything else, the minister held up his hand for silence. "It seems we have much to discuss, but before we do, I suggest the students be dismissed to return home for their daily chores."

A groan of disappointment rumbled from the knot of boys standing along the outer wall. Will grumbled, "Every time something happens, we be told to do our chores."

"Come on, Will. At least there's no homework and I can get caught up."

Outside, they mounted and rode toward the trail.

Arriving at Will's house, the two boys paused, "What do ye think will be the outcome of the meeting?" asked Caleb.

"I don't know, maybe we'll have to start training for the militia," said Will. "A war would surely get rid of the heathens."

"Come on, Will, 'tis hard to believe

there'll be any trouble after the near five score years we English and the Wampanoags have lived together."

"I keep telling ye, Caleb, ye can't trust Indians."

Caleb sighed in exasperation, turned Blackie onto the trail, and rode for home. He wondered about Sassamon's message and what would happen to them all. Where was the Indian boy and what was happening to his people? What would they do when they returned to their summer wigwams beyond the fence that marked the Swanzey lands?

XV
TRIAL IN THE WILDERNESS

The festival was over. Moonwoman's brightest light was gone. Now her tiny crescent hardly lit the sky. Niccone's stomach bulged. He was sure he'd never eat again. He looked up as his father approached.

"Come." Kuttiomp walked outside with his son. "Metacom and we of the Council have decided. If trouble comes with the Awuanaguss, we'll need many warriors. You and your friends have been chosen to winter alone. Be ready when Sun God begins to paint the sky. We will begin your journey together."

Niccone's ribcage felt tight. He sucked in a gulp of air.

"You will leave with only your clothing and knife. The child will go. The man will return." Kuttiomp removed his copper pendant. He slipped the looped thong over his son's head and straightened the jewelry, centering it on Niccone's chest. "This will help you as it has helped me," he said, stepping back and looking at his son.

Niccone rubbed the cold piece of copper between his fingers. It felt comforting.

"I know you'll do well." Kuttiomp smiled.

Niccone cleared his throat. "I'll try," he promised.

Later, Niccone lay in the dark, his eyes open staring into nothing. He fingered his pendant. His stomach churned. He swallowed. Where would Kuttiomp take him? How would he manage? Would he survive? He flung himself on his side. His little brother grunted, annoyed by the motion. Niccone turned again, found a comfortable position, and finally slept. In his dream, Niccone wandered deep in the wilderness. Crows yelled to one another, swooping from limb to limb. Swirling winds from their beating wings knocked him down. The birds surrounded him. They picked him up in their beaks and dropped him on a branch just below a giant black bird.

The bird's raucous voice screamed at him, "Why are you in my forest?"

He tried to speak. Nothing came out. The birds pecked at him. They pulled his cloak off. He tried to yell. The huge bird opened his beak and clamped down hard on

Niccone's shoulder, shaking him viciously. He tried to scream and get away. Suddenly the giant crow dropped him. Niccone looked below to see what had frightened the bird. A huge gray wolf stood growling menacingly. Niccone fell spinning and twirling in silent terror.

"Niccone. Wake up," Kuttiomp shook Niccone's shoulder once more, "Come, it is time to go."

Niccone sat up and stared at his father. "What?" He was relieved to hear his own voice, and realize that he had been dreaming

"Sun God beckons," said Kuttiump.

Niccone dressed quickly. Ottucke handed him a steaming bowl. He wasn't hungry, but he ate anyway. Finishing, he patted Shannuke who twitched in his sleep and rolled into a tight little ball under the furs, missing his brother's warm body. Niccone hugged his mother.

Ottucke wiped a tear from her cheek. "May the animals always be in your traps," she said, hugging him back.

He followed his father into the greyness of the winter dawn. Outside the palisade, he stood still while Kuttiomp tied a leather blindfold on him. He felt a cord knotted around his waist. He held onto it for balance as he stumbled and was led away from his familiar home.

In the distance, he heard crows calling to each other. Far away, he heard a wolf's howl echoing in the silence of the winter sky. He shivered.

Led like a puppy dragged by its master, he trotted along the unknown trail. The early morning cold disappeared, and the winter sun warmed his body. The two of them crossed open valleys and waded through icy streams. The smell from the sea disappeared, replaced by deep woods odors.

Finally the line went slack. "Wait," he called to his father.

"I'll look for you at corn planting, son." Kuttiomp's footsteps receded into silence.

He was frightened. He sat down, feeling the dead leaves on the ground beneath him. Why had his father made the blindfold knot so tight? His head ached with the pressure. He pried at the knot with numb fingers. Tears filled his eyes but couldn't run down his cheeks. What if wolves found him? His fingers were getting stiff. His hand brushed his new pendant. He fingered it, then tried again to untie the blindfold. He loosened it. With one final tug, he tore the hateful thing from his head and started to fling it away. 'Wait. I can make a pouch out of this,' he thought. He tucked it in his belt, rubbed his eyes to clear his vision, and looked skyward. Soon Sun God would pull his light from the sky.

He climbed a tall oak. In the distance, he could see a river flowing through a valley. Descending quickly, he pushed through the forest. The exertion brought warmth to his frigid body. He hurried to the winding waters. It was getting dark as he dug out a hollow in the muddy bank and tucked himself inside, heaping moist earth around his body. As the warmth spread into his mud home, he thought of the turtle. He slept.

XVI
NICCONE'S NEW NAME

Sun God's morning rays touched his face. He awoke, pulled himself out of his mud blanket, and plunged into the icy river. Emerging moments later, he rubbed himself briskly with his soggy breechclout, wrung out his leggings and moccasins and put them on. He climbed up the embankment and stood on high ground. His stomach ached. He ignored his cramps. He climbed another tree, spotted a high steep hill covered with granite outcroppings, and set off toward the mount.

The sun was directly overhead when he arrived. His dried clothing felt warm. Reaching the cliffs, he climbed quickly to a ledge half way up. He poked his head cautiously inside a small cave. He smiled. It was deep enough to keep out the winter snows and large enough to store supplies. A small opening at the top let in a shaft of sunlight. He scooped dead leaves scattered about the face of the cliff and stuffed them inside the opening. Then he scrambled to the forest below and began gathering dead branches, dried grasses and fallen tree limbs. He brought them to the cave and continued collecting into the afternoon.

Just before Sun God left the sky, he discovered groundnut vines crawling along the base of the cliff. He used a stick to unearth the round succulent tubers. Unwrapping his blindfold, he filled it full of the nourishing food and carried it back to his new home. He made several trips and brought all he could find back to the cave.

Inside, Niccone used his knife to make a bow and drill shaft. He took a small stone and used it as a cap. Using a thong from his moccasin as a bowstring, he tied it to a supple stick, making a bow. He twisted the bowstring tightly around the straight shaft, placed the cap on top, and began pulling the bow back and forth. Slowly the friction from the twirling shaft created puffs of smoke in a pile of tinder he'd made from dried leaves and twigs. A moment later, flames erupted. He added more wood. The heat felt good. The flames ate through the twilight darkness. Niccone spread some groundnuts to roast at the edge of the fire. He ate some, banked the fire with green wood, and slid into his bed of leaves pulling his cloak over him. The soft fur tickled his cheek. He thought of home. Snow trickled from the small opening above. He slept.

Much later, he woke shivering. A few embers glowed in the firepit. He crawled out from under his deerskin cloak. Groping in the dark, he added small twigs and branches to the red coals. Smoke curled in his nostrils and watered his eyes. He waited for yellow flames to clear the darkness. They leapt forward and outlined the wood as they crackled and ate the limbs. Smoke wafted toward the opening above and the firelight flickered on the cave walls, creating shadowy monsters of orange and red.

In the firelight, he looked toward the cave opening and gasped. The entrance was blocked with snow. He crawled toward it and began digging. His fingers grew numb. He warmed them over the fire. He ate some of the roasted groundnuts and rested.

He added only enough wood to keep the fire from going out and continued his routine of digging, resting, and feeding the fire. Pale light mixed with snow filtered in from above and he knew Sun God fought the Snow God trying to rule the sky. Later, when the cave grew black except for the small glow in the firepit, he piled green wood on the embers and covered himself with leaves and his cloak once again. Two times a pale Sun God brushed his face and wakened him, but the snow kept falling. He drank melted snow from a puddle. The groundnuts were all gone. He grew weaker. The storm continued. He woke to dig and feed the fire. Sun God left for the fourth time, and he slept.

It was light again. He heard a noise and looked toward the entrance. He rubbed his eyes. He stared. A huge grey wolf, its mouth dripping blood from an animal clutched in its jaws, stood silently at the opening. Helplessly, Niccone watched the wolf crawl slowly inside. Terrified, he felt himself slipping into unconsciousness.

Much later, a shaft of bright sunlight flickered on his face. He studied the reds and yellows making patterns on the back of his eyelids. Suddenly he remembered. He jolted upright. He looked all around. The cave was empty. He climbed out of his pile

Ontaquos, the Wolf

of leaves. Then he saw it. A partially eaten rabbit lay at the nearly cleared entrance. Niccone, grabbed a leg, gnawed its flesh and swallowed the meat in huge gulps. He felt strength flow into his body. He chewed more meat from the rabbit and thrust it onto the embers to roast. The flesh began to sizzle. He grabbed it and chewed ravenously. Its succulent juices ran down his arm. He licked the fat from his forearm and stuffed himself.

He wondered about the wolf. Why hadn't it attacked him? Suddenly he knew. This was his totem! His protector was *ONTAQUOS*, the Wolf.

He said his new name softly, "Ontaquos."

He crawled to the exit, pushed through the snow, and stepped into the bright sunshine. He shouted, "I am Ontaquos! I shall survive!"

He heard the words reverberate throughout the forest. Far off in the distance, a wolf answered his call.

XVII
A SECOND ENCOUNTER

Ontaquos traveled quietly through the thick, leafy woods. He slipped among the shadows of huge trees, his lean, tawny figure blending in with the forest. He understood the signs and sounds of the wilderness. Animal tracks, bird migrations, secrets of water creatures, all had become part of his lore. He could find succulent spring shoots and edible roots and plants. He'd learned the proper stones to make his tools, and he knew the trees to use for shelter, weapons and utensils.

Now he paced himself, jogging along the trail, looking for the familiar signs of the Wampanoag. The back of his neck prickled at a loon's call. He answered and followed the sound. In a small lake, the loon called again, and Ontaquos chuckled as he watched the bird swim lazily in the warm spring sun.

It felt good to be heading toward his own bay country after the long winter and chilly springtime of the Inland People's territory.

Several hours later, he stopped to inspect

an empty Wampanoag campsite. Nets, sinkers, and drying racks had been neatly stored for the next fishing season. Huge, blackened firepits indicated an excellent catch. His mouth watered when he thought of fresh roasted fish sizzling over coals on their bed of green twigs. Ottucke always cooked it just right. He poked around and found storage pits carefully weighted with stones and logs. Hundreds of fish had been smoked and stored for the long winter months that lay ahead. No creature would steal this food.

Ontaquos turned and headed for his summer village. He crossed the small streams easy to ford at the headwaters of the five rivers. Following the path, he brushed invisible cobwebs from his face and bare arms, knowing the spiders would spin their webs again the next day.

He came to a small clearing overlooking the bay. He rested. Sun God seared the earth with his rays. Moon Woman had shaken her stars from her night sky. The sparkling lights shimmered in the bay waters. They glittered and danced when the wind blew, and they gamboled in the waves, waiting for her to call them back when Sun God left the world to sleep. Sighing at the beauty of his beloved bay, Ontaquos plunged back onto the trail that led toward home. A few isolated English farms separated him from the fence that marked his peoples' land.

He heard a foraging deer rustling in the brush. Rubbing his pendant between his fingers, he said a quick prayer to Kiehtan and crept toward the sound. Keeping downwind of the animal, he dropped to one knee, silently placing an arrow notch into his bowstring. He pulled back slowly, stretching the sinew string to its limit. His ear was tuned to the deer's noise. Ontaquos sighted along his arrow shaft. The deer pranced into view. Ontaquos let the arrow fly. The deer, startled by a new noise, had turned and fled.

The speeding arrow flew to its mark and struck the forward haunch of a stray cow that had ambled onto the path. The cow dropped to the ground, its bellowing screams echoing through the trees.

Ontaquos rushed toward the fallen animal. He knew that Longknives often whipped or jailed Wampanoags for injuring cattle. Reaching the animal, he pulled his arrow out of the huge muscle. The cow mooed in fright and pain. Ontaquos searched for and found a thick wad of spider webbing. He thrust it into the wound. He soaked a handful of new green moss in a nearby spring and applied this as well. The bleeding stopped. He examined the cow. No bones were broken. Its eyes rolled in surprise and shock. Ontaquos' gentle voice soothed the frightened beast and she stopped struggling.

Kneeling beside the animal, Ontaquos heard crows' raucous warnings screaming of another intruder. Ontaquos leapt into the underbrush and hid. He clutched his knife.

A young Englishman dressed in leather pants, linen shirt, cotton stockings, and heavy boots came around the bend.

Ontaquos grinned, crawled out of his hiding place and jumped in front of the startled boy. Holding up his hand, he said quickly, "Netop."

His heart pounding, Caleb stopped, eyed the Wampanoag in the path, and exclaimed with relief and recognition, "Netop."

Both boys laughed. Ontaquos led his friend to the wounded animal. He took a stick and began drawing. First he outlined the figure of a deer, then he drew a bow and arrow. Finally he sketched the cow.

Puzzled at first, Caleb studied the figures and then realized what had happened. He nodded his head in understanding. Ontaquos looked relieved.

The two young men bent over the wounded animal. Between them, they shoved, prodded, and forced her to stand. She wobbled unsteadily, then swayed forward. Caleb grinned at Ontaquos and followed his cow along the path to his farm. Ontaquos stood on the path and watched the boy and his cow head for home. He saw the Awuanaguss turn back once to raise his hand in farewell before disappearing around the bend.

Ontaquos waved and then followed his path in the wilderness toward home.

Caleb and Ontaquos with the stray cow

XVIII
HOMECOMING

Nearing his village, Ontaquos heard a
loon's call. He returned the signal. A sentry
stepped from his hiding place on the trail
and waved Ontaquos on. Ontaquos traveled
along the edge of the bay and climbed
steadily to the top of the mount. He walked
to the Council House. For the first time, he
stepped inside.

A group of men sat cross-legged on fur-
covered benches. Smoke from their long-
stemmed Awuanaguss clay pipes mixed with
the blue-grey mist of the firepits. He stood
silently before his elders. His father sat next
to Metacom.

The Medicine Man was the first to speak.
"Here is yet another of our young men
returning from his wintering. We shall have
many new warriors."

Metacom said, "Good. We'll need them
all if the Longknives accuse me of the murder
of the-one-who-did-the-writing."

Ontaquos forced himself not to think of
Sassamon's name. He wondered what had

happened to Metacom's interpreter.

Metacom turned toward Kuttiomp. "Your son did well with his wintering."

Ontaquos looked at his father. Kuttiomp appraised his son. Ontaquos' tall, sinewy, strong body proved he could survive in the wilderness. Kuttiomp admired Ontaquos' beautifully carved bow and birchbark quiver case full of well fletched arrows.

Metacom spoke. "We welcome back our sons and prepare to initiate them into the Warrior Society. You will stay with the others until your initiation is completed. Afterwards, you'll be presented to the tribe."

Ontaquos turned to accompany a beckoning guard. Following along, he wondered who else had returned. They left the village and traveled along a hidden path. The forest thickened. Finally they entered a small clearing deep in the woods.

Ontaquos whooped with delight and ran toward Whauksus. The two friends pounded each other and jumped with excitement as they greeted one another. Other boys gathered around. They all welcomed Ontaquos and talked excitedly of their adventures.

Finally the two friends drifted off and sat on a fallen log in the warm sunlight. For a while neither spoke. Then Ontaquos turned to his friend. "I had my vision," he said quietly. "It was of Ontaquos, The Wolf. He came to me in a cave. He shared a rabbit and saved me from starving."

His friend nodded. "I am now Tomaquog, the Beaver. If it had not been for him, I'd have frozen to death. I followed him and found a dam full of beavers. They gave themselves to me. There were enough to feed me well and make a warm blanket cloak as well. That's how I survived the winter ice."

"I'm glad." Ontaquos paused and then said softly, "Tomaquog."

They both smiled. It was good to be together again.

XIX
WARRIORS AT LAST

Ontaquos stood in the center of the village near the Council House with the others. Tomaquog stood next to him. Ontaquos touched his cheekbone. It hurt, but he was proud to wear his new Wolf tattoo. Tomaquog's raw, red beaver design stood out on his cheek. Ontaquos winked at Tomaquog when he touched his face and winced. They both smiled. To have gone through the initiation successfully made them blood brothers as well as best friends.

Ontaquos looked at the gathering crowd. Shannuke danced on one foot, then the other waiting impatiently to greet him. He now wore a breechclout. How many moons had he worn it? Ontaquos wondered.

Ottucke stood with the women. She smiled. Her lovely face and dark eyes expressed the joy she felt. Ottucke is a good name for her, thought Ontaquos. She is much like a deer.

All the Wampanoags were waiting for the-ceremony-of-the-new-Warriors to begin.

Warriors moved aside and licked their
forearms in greeting as Metacom and his
advisors strode to the center of the gathering.
Metacom wore full regalia. A wampum
headband circled his head. More wampum
beadwork crossed his shoulders and wrapped
around his waist, glistening white and purple
in the sunlight. His crippled hand rested on
the handle of his hunting knife tucked into
its sheath on his belt. His good hand
grasped his flintlock, its butt resting on the
ground before him. The long steel barrel
flashed in the sunlight.

He spoke. "Here are our young Warriors.
They have learned to live alone in the forest.
They know the secrets of the Warrior
Society. They will protect and defend the
people of the Wampanoag Nation." He
pointed to the villagers as he spoke. "Many
things have happened since the Awuanaguss
arrived so many moons ago when my father
was strong and leader to our people."

Ontaquos tried to imagine Metacom as a
child. He couldn't.

"We have seen our lands changed into
English villages and towns. Their animals
roam our forests and trample our corn fields."

Everyone nodded.

Metacom continued, "They make us live by their rules and punish us with imprisonment and fines and whippings in their public squares. When we complain of their theft or unlawful use of our lands, they say we have no rights. They tell us their King James laws are just and we must not question."

Kuttiomp and the other Council members vigorously nodded their heads in agreement.

"They give us English names and call me King Philip, but I am not a King to them. Right now in the place we call Umpame and they call Plimoth, there's a trial. Three of our warriors are accused of murdering one of our own, The-one-who-spoke-for-me."

Ontaquos blanked out Sassamon's name. He remembered him as a kind man with much knowledge and wisdom. It was sad to think of him dead.

"They may even accuse me of his death."

Shouts of "We will kill them!" echoed among the Warriors.

Metacom smiled at them but cautioned, "You must wait for me to give the signal.

There is much to be done and much to prepare."

Turning toward the young men standing together in the center of the circle he said, "Here are our newest young fighting men. They have endured hardship and difficult testing. None has failed." Approaching each one in turn, he spoke to them and then, announcing their new Warrior name presented each to the onlookers.

He came to Ontaquos and clasped his shoulders. Ontaquos felt Metacom's crippled hand, gnarled and twisted from an exploding gun that had blown up when he was a boy.

Metacom said very softly, "You are the son of one of my leading generals. He is an honorable, brave man and you are much like him. You will be asked to do many things. I know you will do them well. I welcome you."

"I will do whatever you ask." Ontaquos felt a fierce pride. He knew he would be willing to die for this man.

Metacom's voice called strongly and clearly, "And this is Ontaquos, son of Kuttiomp." Everyone cheered. Metacom continued down the line of young men.

Finally when the last one had been recognized and welcomed, one of the older Warriors yelled, "It's time to feast and celebrate with our new brothers."

Everyone rushed forward. Families enveloped their sons. Ontaquos scooped up Shannuke, tossing him high, laughing at the shrieks echoing skyward in the late afternoon sun. Once on the ground, the little boy grabbed his brother's hand and pulled him toward their wigwam. Ottucke hugged him and then pointed to the sleeping platform. He carefully examined the beautiful new moccasins, held up the soft, tan leggings, and brushed his hand across his new breechclout with its quilled design along the outer edges.

He laughed when Shannuke told him how he'd clubbed a big rattlesnake high in the rocks behind the cornfields. Ottucke had made it into a beautiful belt. Ontaquos knew how frightened Shannuke had been stalking the slithery reptile, and he hugged him.

A shadow fell across the sleeping platform. Ontaquos turned to see Kuttiomp standing in the doorway. In his left hand he held a flintlock. His other hand held a powderhorn and bullet pouch. He held them toward his son. "Here. You have earned these. After the feasting and celebrating is over, I'll teach you how to use them."

Ontaquos took them. He held the barrel, then put the stock against his shoulder, aiming down the end of the gunbarrel. "I wonder when I'll use this against a man," he said.

XX
THE WAR PARTY

"Don't tarry! There's too much work for ye to be running off with your friends."

Caleb nodded and mounted Blackie. He dug his heels into his horse's belly and galloped down the path, followed by Lad.

The cool shade of the green forest felt good. He slowed Blackie to a walk. Crows cawed to one another. Seagulls screamed their lonely cry, circling high above the forest floor. Caleb brushed the cobwebs from his face and swatted at buzzing flies. It was good to be here alone. Green leaves rustled, birds flitted, and dapple sunshine blinked through the thick foliage. He traveled leisurely, enjoying the sounds and smells, finally emerging into the open fields that led to Will's house.

"Ho, Caleb," Will hollered from the edge of the field.

Caleb reined up and waited for Will, who came running toward him, "Where be ye going?" asked Will, wiping sweat from his brow.

"The miller's for cornmeal."

"When I finish this field, I be done for a bit. Why don't ye help me and then we both can go fishing?"

"I'm not supposed to tarry," said Caleb.

"If ye help me, ye'll be working, and fishing means food for the table. Is that not work as well?" Will grinned.

Caleb laughed, "Ye'd be right." he said. "Where's another hoe?" He slipped from Blackie's back and followed Will, leading Blackie behind him. Caleb hitched Blackie to the hitching post in the shade.

A half an hour later, they hung the hoes on a hook in the barn and grabbed the fishing poles leaning in a corner. The two of them followed the trail that led to a rocky beach. Caleb and Will, followed by Lad, climbed over the rocks and walked until they arrived at a small beach at the edge of the shore. Smashing a mussel, they baited their hooks with the mussels, adjusted cork floats, and let out the line. Lad bounded into the water, splashing and paddling toward the floats.

"No!" yelled Caleb.

Lad turned and swam toward them,

waded ashore, and shook all over them.

"Go lie down!" both boys shouted in unison. Lad crawled up the bank and grunted loudly as he flung himself onto the ground. Caleb and Will shoved their poles into boulders along the edge of the shore and added more stones to prop them up. Then they climbed the bank and settled under an old oak tree near Lad, who thumped his tail at them.

"Sure is peaceful," said Will, stripping a stem of grass with his teeth and chewing on the tender end.

"Aye," answered Caleb, stretching out and closing his eyes.

Waves slapped against the shore, swishing around the huge boulders and gurgling over the smaller stones that lay among the eel grass. A southwest wind rustled leaves above the boys' heads, keeping the deer flies away. Suddenly Lad raised his head. From deep within his chest an almost imperceptible growl rumbled. Caleb sprang at him, grabbing his muzzle. "Quiet, Lad," he whispered, patting the dog and looking all around.

Will shook Caleb's shoulder quietly and

pointed to a shadow in the forest beyond where they lay. In the distance, a dozen Indians were silently following one another in single file. Their heads were shaved except for a strip of hair running down the middle of their scalps from forehead to neck. Painted designs covered their faces and bodies. Each one carried a musket. Bullet pouches and powderhorns hung from their belts.

Caleb and Will watched silently as the group soundlessly followed along the trail that led toward the fence marking King Philip's territory. Caleb held Lad's muzzle firmly. He wrapped his other arm around the dog's body, holding him securely.

Long after the Indians had disappeared, Caleb and Will and Lad lay still. Finally Will whispered to Caleb, "Did ye see how they looked? 'Tis a War Party, Caleb."

"It surely looks like one," said Caleb. "But maybe 'tis a hunting party."

"Not with all that paint. Come on," said Will. "We've got to tell our folks." The two of them scrambled down the embankment and gathered their fishing poles. Lad chased after them. Caleb and Will hurried along the trail. Back at Will's farm, Caleb grabbed Blackie's reins, mounted him quickly and wheeled him back onto the trail. He urged Blackie along the trail to his farm.

In his yard he dismounted hastily. Lad dropped wearily onto the ground and crawled under a wagon.

"Father! Mother!"

Abigail rushed from the milk house and Tom from the corn fields. When Caleb had finished, his mother spoke. "Well, I be staying here no matter what those heathens do." She put her hands on her hips and stood defiantly looking off to the Wampanoag lands. Then her gaze shifted to the little cemetery under the apple tree. Caleb looked at the tiny markers of his brothers and sisters. None had survived beyond infancy.

Tom patted Abigail. "Don't worry. We won't leave unless we have to."

Abigail turned away quickly.

Caleb saw the tears. He put his arm around his mother. " 'Twill be all right, Mother."

She wiped her eyes on her apron and turned toward the house. "Come," she said.

" 'Tis time for the evening meal."

With a final glance toward the Mount, they entered the house.

After supper Tom said, "We'll leave Lad to guard the farm outside tonight. Fix him a place to sleep under the wagon." Tom took down a new gun from the wall hooks and handed it to Caleb. "And, Caleb, ye might take yer gun with ye when ye be about the farmyard."

"Did ye say my gun?" Caleb grinned at Tom.

"Aye," smiled Tom, "Ye be ready now."

XXI
DETAINED BY WARRIORS

Several days later, Tom called, "Caleb, come! We be going to town. Some horses have strayed into Wampanoag lands. I be beckoned to go with the owners to speak to the Wampanoags. I want ye with me."

Caleb dropped his hoe and ran to saddle Blackie.

"No," said Tom. "We'll take the wagon and all go into town. I fear for yer mother here all alone these days. Don't alarm her, but tell her to get ready to go with us."

Caleb went inside and told her. While Abigail prepared, he took down the guns, powder, and bullet pouches and brought them to the wagon. They drove off. Lad gazed at the receding wagon with sad eyes, then plopped in the shade on the granite doorstep and waited.

At the Common, townsfolk had gathered. Caleb helped his mother down from the wagon. She joined a throng of women who stood watching the men collect in a close group.

Reverend Myles raised his hand for

silence. " 'Twould be best if only a few men go into the Wampanoag lands. We don't want them to think we be wanting trouble. Since Tom speaks some Wampanoag, he's a logical leader."

"Aye," the men agreed.

"And leave yer weapons here," Reverend Myles cautioned.

Tom chose Job Winslow, and two others along with Caleb.

"Why Caleb?" Will's father asked.

"He be friendly with one of the younger Wampanoags," Tom answered. He handed their weapons to Will's father. "We'll be needing these on our journey back to the farm."

The five of them got in the cart. Tom guided Blackie toward the Wampanoag lands. Caleb waved at a white-faced Abigail. She closed her eyes in a silent prayer.

The woods enveloped them. They finally reached the fence that marked the Indian lands. Tom crossed over and called, "What Cheer, Netop!"

They waited.

A shadow slipped among the trees. Then another. Soon a dozen warriors surrounded the cart. One of them grabbed the reins and tugged. Blackie whinnied in pain.

Tom leapt out, "Leave him be!" he commanded in the Indians' language.

Startled to hear Wampanog words coming from an Englishman, the warrior dropped the reins.

The Swanzey men and Caleb stepped down, forming a semi-circle around Blackie. The warriors moved forward and pushed them away from the cart.

"Let's take them prisoners. We can hold them the way they are holding our people in Plimoth," said the one of the Wampanoags.

Tom answered in Wampanoag. "Your people are being tried for the murder of Sassamon. We have done nothing to harm you."

"You steal our lands. You jail our men. Your animals trample our cornfields," one of the Indians yelled.

The others chanted, "Yes! Yes! Let's take them prisoners."

Warriors grabbed the Swanzey men and threw them to the ground.

An Indian grabbed Caleb and pulled his hair. "This would make a fine scalp," he exclaimed to his friends. He unsheathed his knife.

Caleb hollered. Tom tried to lunge for the Indian but was held down.

XXII
THE PENDANT

Ontaquos and Tomaquog travelled along the trail that led along Awuanaguss lands. Hunting had been sparse and they followed the marked lands between the Wampanoags and the English on their way back to their main camp.

Suddenly Ontaquos stopped. "Look," He pointed to the men who'd gathered at the fence. "Our Warriors detain Awuanaguss. What are they doing in our territory?"

"Let's go see," said Tomaquog.

The two friends approached the group. They saw warriors holding Englishmen down on the ground.

Ontaquos saw a young Awuanaguss straddled by a warrior. A knife flashed in the sunlight Ontaquos looked at the golden hair held by the warrior.

"Tomaquog, go get Metacom!" Ontaquos plunged into the group of men and grabbed the warrior's knife hand. "Wait!" He stood between the attacker and Caleb. "Netop," he said softly to Caleb.

Caleb coughed. "Netop," he whispered recognizing his friend.

"This is my friend. I don't want him harmed." Ontaquos removed his pendant and placed it around Caleb's neck.

The warriors looked confused.

A shout distracted them all. They looked toward the Wampanoag lands. In the distance, Caleb and the others watched a tall figure wearing an English shirt, breechclout, and wampum belts stride toward them. Powerful-looking Wampanoags surrounded him.

" 'Tis Metacom," whispered Tom. "Let's hope he's still friendly."

"What's going on?" Metacom demanded, joining the group.

An Indian stepped forward. "We have come to fight the Longknives. Let us kill these people and drive all the others from their homes." He grabbed his tomahawk.

"Put it down!" Metacom commanded, then turned to Tom. "What do you do here?"

"We mean no harm. We just want our horses."

"No," shouted the Indian who had

detained them. "These animals are here on our lands. They belong to us."

Other warriors nodded in agreement.

"I am Sachem of the Wampanoags. You will do what I say," said Metacom forcefully.

Caleb stared at the tall, imposing figure. "What be happening?" he whispered to his father.

"They be deciding," Tom answered.

Metacom stood apart with his councilors. "We do not want trouble before our time of choosing," he cautioned.

The glint of copper caught his eye. He approached Caleb, stood before him, then grasped the pendant around his neck, "Where did you get this?" He yanked on the pendant. Caleb winced. The wrench thrust him forward.

"I gave it to him. He is my friend." Ontaquos came and stood next to Caleb.

Metacom asked Ontaquos, "Why have you given this Englishman your special pendant?"

"We met and shared a wildcat we'd both hunted. And he helped me when I was in the Englishman's territory and could have been charged with a crime."

Metacom smiled and grasped Caleb's shoulders firmly. "You have proven to be a fine friend."

Caleb looked at Tom to translate. "He says ye've been a fine friend."

Metacom spoke to Tom. "You are free to go with your horses. Do not let them roam here again. You have seen how my warriors feel about you coming into our lands."

"Aye, we'll not let it happen again," Tom said. "But ye'd be wise to keep your warriors from doing anything that would cause us to call for troops from Plimoth."

"I shall see what happens with the trial," Metacom answered.

Ontaquos looked at Caleb. "Netop," he said.

Caleb smiled and rubbed the pendant. "Netop," he replied.

The Swanzey men tied the horses to their wagon, and clamored aboard. Tom smiled at Caleb, who climbed up with the others. When Tom saw them all safely in the wagon, he gave orders to drive off.

XXIII
SABBATH MEETING

The following Sunday, Caleb harnessed Blackie to the cart and led him to the farmhouse.

"Hurry, Caleb, we'll be late for the Sabbath Meeting." Abigail climbed in. Her eyes traveled around the familiar sights of the farm, then looked off to the forest beyond.

Tom signaled Blackie, and Caleb jumped into the back of the cart. Tom cocked his head and Caleb slid his hand beneath a thin layer of new hay in the bottom of the cart. He fingered the triggers and smoothed his palm along the gun stocks hidden beneath. He nodded to his father. Tom drove the cart onto the trail. Caleb rubbed his copper pendant.

Arriving at the Meeting House, Tom stopped and Caleb helped his mother down. She went inside. Tom drove to the hitching post. Both Tom and Caleb grabbed their weapons, and joined the other armed men standing outside listening to Job Winslow.

He nodded to Tom and Caleb. "I be telling the others my home was looted yesterday when we were out in the fields."

"Be there any damage?" asked Tom.

"A few things overturned, some food taken, but most important, my powderhorn be missing."

"Who do ye think did it?" Tom asked.

" 'Twas Indians. We've sent to Plimoth for troops."

Caleb nudged Will, who had approached the group with his father as Job Winslow spoke. "They be bringing in soldiers," he whispered to his friend. Mr. Winslow's place was looted yesterday."

"Heathens be nothing but trouble," Will whispered back.

The bell rang for service to begin, and Caleb followed his father and the others inside. Everyone stacked their muskets just inside the main door.

Caleb sat next to Tom, who had squeezed into their bench. Will and his father sat in front of them. Caleb studied Will's hair. Swirls of dark waves spread in different directions. He wondered what his own hair looked like. Would his hair and scalp and

Will's and all the others' hang from an Indian's belt? What would he and his family find when they returned home from the Sabbath service? What would the troops do when they arrived from Plimoth? He fingered his pendant and tried to concentrate on the sermon. He couldn't.

XXIV
THE RAID

Ontaquos and Tomaquog sat near the outdoor cooking pot. They had dipped their spoons and filled their stomachs.

"I wonder when we'll hear about the trial." Ontaquos scratched his stomach.

Tomaquog rolled over on his back just as Sun God appeared from behind a small, puffy, white cloud. Tomaquog squinted and looked away. "Perhaps now. Look!" He pointed to a sweaty, panting messenger loping along the path to the Council House.

The two of them hurriedly joined the throng of gathering Warriors. They all stood waiting silently outside. Finally Tomaquog nudged Ontaquos with his elbow. Ontaquos nodded, watching Metacom approach the group. His Council Members and Advisors stood behind him.

Metacom spoke to the crowd, "Our brothers have been called guilty. We shall see what the Longknives say to me. If they accuse me of ordering the death of the-one-who-writes, we will fight."

"LET'S FIGHT NOW!"

Ontaquos and the others turned to see a warrior painted for battle. He aimed his gun skyward and pulled the trigger. The flame flashed and the gun roared. Someone started drumming and the Warriors' voices began War chants.

Metacom shouted his answer. "Not yet. Be ready but wait for my signal."

The Warrior with his flintlock grumbled. Ontaquos and Tomaquog drifted away and sat on a cedar mat near the cook pot.

"Our men grow restless. Some of them went to some of the Longknives' houses at the edge of town. They brought back a nice powder horn."

Tomaquog jumped up. "Let's go see an English house. I've never been in one."

"Neither have I." Ontaquos slapped Tomaquog's shoulder. "This is the day the Longknives call 'Sabbath'. They'll all be in their Sabbath House."

Tomaquog grinned. "Maybe we can get some English sweet food." He rubbed his stomach in anticipation. "That would be worth the trip."

Ontaquos and Tomaquog at the farmhouse

Ontaquos nodded. "I'll get my gun. You get yours and we'll go."

He raced to his wigwam and returned. The two young men ran along the path leading from the camp. Much later, they stopped by a thick brush fence.

"I hate this fence," said Tomaquog.

"The Longknives say it's to keep their sheep and cattle and horses from straying into our lands," answered Ontaquos.

"That's what they say," snorted Tomaquog. "More likely it's to keep us penned up like their sheep."

Ontaquos laughed. "You're not very fond of our English neighbors."

"Are you?" asked Tomaquog.

"Not really, but remember the one who wears my pendant? I sometimes wonder if there aren't more like him."

"A fine Warrior you are." Tomaquog raced ahead.

Ontaquos laughed again and spurted forward to catch up.

He flicked his hand at Tomaquog and brushed his arm. "Don't worry, Netop, I'll fight better than anyone if we go to war."

The two hurdled the fence gracefully and traveled toward the farms on the outskirts of their lands. They emerged into a cleared field and dropped down behind a stone fence.

"This one looks deserted. Let's go inside and see what we can find," said Tomaquog.

They approached the house cautiously. They peeked inside. It was empty. They unlatched the door, pushed it open, and stepped inside. They found several large wooden chests and began opening lids and pulling out blankets, pillows, clothing, and utensils.

Tomaquog found a woman's hat and put it on. They both laughed. He searched for a looking glass. Suddenly he noticed a small white bowl on a table near the fireplace. A spoon handle stuck through a hole in the cover. He lifted the lid. Inside, white granules filled it nearly to the top. He shouted to Ontaquos, grabbed the spoon, scooped it full, and popped it into his mouth. With a gasp he clutched his throat and spit out the soggy white mound. He wiped his mouth with the hat and threw it on the floor. He searched wildly for something to drink.

Ontaquos stared in amazement. He gingerly dipped his moistened finger into the powder. Touching it to his tongue, he recoiled at the awful taste of salt. He hooted at Tomaquog, who was throwing things wildly about searching for something to drink. Feeling sorry for his friend, Ontaquos finally found a wooden bucket, its leather lid tightly in place. He pried off the cover, tasted its contents, and laughingly handed the cider to his friend.

Tomaquog gulped it down. Then he grabbed the salt bowl and threw it on the floor.

Neither of them heard the door latch lift quietly.

Suddenly a dark-haired English lad hurled himself into the room. Tomaquog and Ontaquos grabbed their guns, pushed the startled boy out of the way, and fled through the open door.

Will dropped to one knee, aimed his flintlock, and fired. One of the Indians stumbled and fell. The other turned back to help him. Will reloaded.

Ontaquos hoisted Tomaquog onto his shoulders and disappeared into the forest.

"Will, are ye all right?" shouted his father, running from the barn.

XXV
THE FIRST CASUALTY

Ontaquos laid his friend down. "Tomaquog, why did it have to be you?"

Tomaquog smiled weakly, "Remember what our Wise Man predicted. He said the one who draws the first blood will lose the war. It's worth this wound." He struggled to breathe, then whispered. "No more Awuanaguss towns. Our lands back as they were." He groaned.

Ontaquos rolled a wad of thick spider webbing and pushed it into the wound in Tomaquog's side. Then he carried him along the trail to the camp. A sentry challenged him. He trilled the whippoorwill call and hollered, "Come! Help me."

They carried Tomaquog to the Medicine Man. Warriors crushed against one another to hear what had happened. When they heard how Tomaquog had been attacked, they prepared for war.

Ontaquos stayed with Tomaquog. The Healer began chanting as he laid out his medicines. He mixed special herbs and powders and offered them to Tomaquog. Alternately ministering to the wounds and chanting and appealing to the spirits that watch over Man, the Healer worked unceasingly. Tomaquog's chest rose and fell. Each breath took longer. The Healer's chanting grew louder. The Medicine Man worked feverishly, applying all the remedies he knew.

After many hours, Ontaquos finally stood and stretched his cramped muscles. Yawning, he faced the East. Sun God sent a thin light blue stripe to warn Moonwoman of his coming. Next, he painted a narrow line of pale pink just above the blue. Moonwoman began gathering her stars, throwing handfuls into the bay below. She ambled across the darkness. Her lantern weakened. Sun God swaggered into his celestial territory with a searing flame of orange, casting his reflection onto Tomaquog's quiet form. Ontaquos turned to look at his friend.

Tomaquog's eyes stared vacant and unseeing. His chest was still. The Medicine Man's shoulders sagged. Ontaquos grabbed his knife and slashed his own arm, letting his blood fall on his lifeless Netop's body. His cries and those of Tomaquog's family filled the village. Everyone joined the mourners.

Metacom arrived, his head shaved, except for the Warrior's center strip. He wore red and black paint on his face. He knelt beside Tomaquog's dead body, his eyes a mixture of sadness and fury.

He rose and faced his people to make the formal speech that was necessary. "It was said by our Wiseman, our Medicine Man, who speaks to our great God, Kiehtan, God of the Southwest where all living things come and go, and where this fallen one has gone, that the one who draws the first blood will lose the war!

"The Longknives have chosen their destiny. We shall strike and drive out all Awunaguss. Victory shall be ours!"

The circle of Warriors shouted in unison, "Death to the Longknives! War to the end!"

Ontaquos, weeping, cradled his dead friend. "I swear to avenge you," he said, putting him down gently. Then raising his bloody fist in the sign of war, he joined the War Dance Circle.

XXVI
AT THE GARRISON

Caleb and Will stood outside Myles' garrison watching the Plimoth troops set up their camp. Swanzey neighbors unloaded their provisions and tended their animals.

"Since 'twas I who shot the heathen, everyone says my family'd be safer at the Bourne garrison in Swanzey. 'Tis larger and stronger and made of stone. Others are going too. Why don't ye come with us?" said Will.

"My parents choose to stay here. When do ye leave?" asked Caleb.

"Now. They've assigned some of the Plimoth soldiers to scout ahead and guard against ambush."

Caleb walked with Will to the group of travelers and soldiers waiting on the Wilderness Trail, "I'll miss ye, Will."

"And I'll miss ye, Caleb." Will grinned.

"Don't worry. With all these soldiers, we'll be back home in a couple of weeks."

"I pray so."

They both looked toward the Indian lands. "I told ye, ye couldn't trust those heathens. When I saw them in my house grabbing and breaking things, I knew I had to shoot."

"Aye, Will, but 'tis a shame we can't talk to King Philip and his people and work things out."

"No one can talk to a heathen. They're not to be trusted. We'd be better off if they were all gone."

"Hold on, Will, 'twas their land before 'twas ours. If it hadn't been for King Philip's father, Massasoit, there'd be no Plimoth, nor Swanzey, nor any other town today."

"Aye, but they sold it to us and every deed was approved by the Governor and his Council so no one could take advantage of them, and they surely were eager to accept the axes and hoes and blankets and wampum we paid them."

"Aye, 'tis true, but the way they kept coming back to their lands for hunting and fishing, maybe they didn't understood the terms."

"If they haven't been able to figure it out after fifty years, there's something wrong."

"Aye, there's something wrong, and it looks like the Wampanoags have decided to do something about it. Be careful on your journey, Will. God knows when we'll meet again."

" 'Twon't take long to teach them a lesson. I've already proved that myself." Will stopped talking when he noticed his father motioning to him.

"God be with ye, Will. I hope we'll all be back home soon," said Caleb patting his friend on the shoulder.

Will hauled himself onto the back of the wagon and cradled his gun in his arm. His hand flashed a quick wave and the small group of villagers, led by the Plimoth troops, headed toward the safety of Bourne garrison.

Caleb stood watching Will and his family's wagon disappear into the curve in the trail.

"Caleb, don't just stand there. Get the livestock penned in the compound. We don't want animals straying off in the middle of the night, confusing us with their sounds of wandering." Tom patted his son's shoulder. "Don't worry about Will. With all these soldiers, "'twon't take long to subdue the uprising."

Caleb and Lad hurried to the compound. Later, Caleb pushed his way into the crowded Myles' garrison house, stepping over bedding and supplies spread on the floor. Abigail cleared a place in the corner. She flapped the quilts out and laid them down for the night. Caleb grabbed a corner of the bedding and she smiled at him as he helped her arrange it.

"Who'd have thought there'd be a war," Caleb said.

"Aye, Caleb, 'tis sad, but the thought of heathens looting and burning our farm fills me with hatred."

"Aye, we've always protected our own," said Caleb, "and we'll do it now, but I wonder if the Quakers in Newport might not be right with their preaching peace for all peoples."

"Nonsense! As long as heathens attack and burn, there'll be no peace for any of us."

Caleb sighed. "Ye'd be right on that." He went to see what else needed to be done outside.

XXVII
NIGHT ATTACK

Caleb stood on a bench, peering into the blackness of the moonless night. His eyes ached with the strain. He lowered his gun, leaning it against the window frame, and rubbed his eyes. He squinted, then, aiming his gun into the darkness, he waited.

"Caleb, do ye see anything?" Noah Wilson from the farm next to Will's whispered from across the room.

"No. Do ye?"

Just then a screeching howl seared the silence and gun fire flashed from the edge of the clearing. Caleb aimed at the sound. He heard the soldiers outside cursing and bellowing orders as they scurried for cover. Caleb watched a second flame erupt and fired at it. He heard another hideous scream and more gunfire. He reloaded and aimed.

From outside came the call, "Come! Get our wounded!" It was the sergeant from the Plimoth Militia. Caleb and Noah rushed to the door along with Tom and two others. Crouching low, they followed the sounds of men's voices, and scurried to the knot of soldiers behind the haystack. Feeling more than seeing in the night blackness, each of them quickly grabbed the wounded soldiers and dragged them to the safety of the garrison. Caleb banged on the door. It was quickly opened by one of the women. Helping hands reached for the wounded men. Caleb looked into the deep brown eyes of a young man, whose face contorted in pain. Caleb pulled the young man inside.

"That could be me", said Caleb softly to himself, as he turned back to the blackness.

More shots and yelling came from the Indians at the edge of the forest, and two more soldiers crumpled. Caleb, Noah, and Tom dragged and carried these wounded men to the safety of the garrison. They slammed the door shut.

Several women hurried to the groaning men and began tearing their aprons to make bandages.

"Tom! Caleb! Be ye all right?" Abigail called as she added wood to the fire to boil water.

"We be fine," said Tom.

When the women finished, Abigail said,

"We be needing a surgeon to tend these men."

"Be there any man willing to go to Rehoboth for the surgeon?" asked Tom.

"Aye," said William Waterman.

"And I too," answered Pardon Sweet. The two of them grabbed their flintlocks, bullet pouches, and powder horns.

"We'll have the soldiers fire at the heathens and we'll shoot from the windows and the gun holes. That should give ye both enough time to get away. God be with ye both," said Tom shaking their hands.

The two men kissed their wives and children and went to the back of the house where they could slip out the rear door. Caleb climbed onto his bench and aimed at the forest. Noah and the others took their positions. Tom crawled from the house to the haystack and told the sergeant what they were planning.

"Ready! Aim! Fire!" Job Winslow commanded from the front window.

Caleb felt the kick from his gun and watched the flames from all the weapons pierce the blackness. He wondered if the night would ever end.

XXVIII
VENGEANCE

Ontaquos lay behind a fallen log with several other Wampanoag Warriors. Kuttiomp crawled to them. "We'll keep the Awuanaguss busy with gunfire, but we cannot attack with all the Longknife soldiers. Someone must follow the trail beyond the house to make sure no one escapes and goes for more soldiers."

"I will go," said Ontaquos.

"And I," said Wawunnes, an older Warrior.

"Good," said Kuttiomp. "We'll fire on the Longknives until Sun God begins to arrive. Then we'll all return to our village."

Ontaquos and Wawunnes silently crept around the building while Kuttiomp and the others screeched and fired at the garrison. Ontaquos and Wawunnes followed a path that led onto the trail. Leaving the Awunaguss house far behind, they finally hid themselves in a rocky mound above the path. They waited.

Suddenly, Ontaquos nudged Wawunnes. Wawunnes tapped Ontaquos' arm. They both held their breath.

Not far from their hiding place they heard two Longknives coming toward them. The Longknives' powder horns banged against their bodies and their bullet pouches rattled.

Ontaquos and Wawunnes waited. The men ran below them. Ontaquos and Wawunnes plunged out of their hiding place and dropped on their enemies. Ontaquos slammed his foe to the ground, grasped his knife, and drove it deeply into the man's chest. He heard him grunt. Ontaquos struck again and the man's body went limp.

Moonwoman came out from behind the clouds. Ontaquos stood up and looked around. Moonlight glistened on the bear grease and bright colors of Wawunnes gleaming body. He stood straddling his motionless enemy sprawled on the ground.

Ontaquos stared down at the two dead Awuanaguss. He thought of Tomaquog. "I've avenged you, my dead friend," he whispered quietly into the night air.

'What Longknife will come after me to retaliate for this life?' he wondered, looking down at the dead Englishman.

His anger left him.

XXIX
BAD NEWS

Caleb sat outside in the shade tossing pebbles aimlessly at an anthill. Tiny ants scurried in all directions, some regrouping to collect the injured while others began repairing the damage. Caleb watched. He thought about the night just past. When he closed his eyes, he saw the face of the young soldier he'd helped rescue. He dreaded another night like the last one. He had tried to sleep when the attack had ended, but groans from the wounded had kept him awake. In the early morning one of the soldiers had died. Caleb had helped dig the grave. He was saddened at the man's death, but relieved it was not the young brown-eyed soldier who now lay bandaged and quiet in the garrison.

Now, Caleb was here in the bright sunshine. He still couldn't sleep. Where were Mr. Waterman and Mr. Sweet? Why hadn't they returned with the surgeon? What had happened to Will? Did Bourne garrison have an Indian attack too? All these thoughts pounded through his brain. His head ached, leaving him exhausted but too agitated to rest.

He leapt up at the sound of horses' hooves on the trail and ran to the knot of people who had gathered to greet the riders.

Three strangers wearing clothing of the Massachusetts Bay Colony reined up. Caleb pushed through the crowd in time to hear the first man say, "I be Captain Savage." He dismounted and handed his reins to a soldier standing near by. "We've ridden from Boston."

One of his companions interrupted. "We'd hoped to intercede and mediate in your Indian dispute, but 'tis too late. There's been too much killing."

"How did ye know of our young soldier who died last night?" asked Tom.

"What soldier? We found two dead men on the Wilderness Trail not far from here," replied Captain Savage.

Cries of anguish came from the wives of the missing men. Abigail and the other women tried to console them.

The third Bay man spoke. "Six more have been killed from Bourne garrison. They'd gone to get food from nearby farms and were ambushed on the trail."

"Who were they?" Everyone looked worried.

"We don't know," answered Captain Savage.

Tom issued orders. "We've got to have more troops. I'll send a message to Plimoth. In the meantime some of us should go with our troops to keep the Wampanoags from escaping from their village on the peninsula at Mauntop. We'll leave enough men here to protect the garrison."

"I'll go," said Caleb.

"No." Tom put his hand on his son's shoulder. "Ye stay to protect yer mother and the others. We'll choose some to go and others to remain. Ye stay for our family."

Caleb nodded, trying not to show his disappointment.

" 'Twon't be long," said Tom, "Once we've surrounded the Wampanoags and blocked their escape route from the peninsula, we'll capture King Philip and then we'll all be able to go home."

"What will happen to King Philip?" asked Caleb.

"Probably be tried for treason in a court at Plimoth," Tom answered. He went inside to get his equipment.

Caleb followed.

XXX
GRUESOME DISCOVERY

While Tom and the others were gone, Caleb and Lad kept busy tending animals. Caleb made sure they were tethered, fed, and watered. He carried buckets from the spring. Lad followed everywhere.

Entering the house, Caleb threaded his way among the crowded residents, nearly stepping on a tiny toddler tottering toward him. Caleb set his pails next to the fireplace and its steaming caldrons of stew. He slipped the yoke from his shoulders and unhooked the buckets, pouring the water carefully into wooden barrels next to the chimney. He smiled reassuringly at his mother and turned to leave.

Abigail stopped stirring the thick stew and brushed aside a loose strand of hair that had plastered itself to her perspiring forehead. "Any word of yer father and the others?" She looked tired and worried.

"No. But 'tis mighty quiet outside. There's no sign of any Wampanoags. New soldiers continue to arrive every day, and word is that there's a company of soldiers building a fort near the Indian fence to keep King Philip from fleeing." He brushed her arm. "Don't worry, Mother. He'll be back soon."

Readjusting his yoke, Caleb turned to leave, bumping into the ample back of a woman bending over her Dutch oven at the edge of the fireplace. He dodged her blow and disappeared around the chimney.

Outside, he saw a young girl holding her long skirts to keep from tripping. She ran toward the house shouting, "The men are coming."

Caleb ran inside. "Mother, the men are coming! I see Father!" Grabbing her hand, he tugged her through the crowd and propelled her beyond the open door.

The men plodded along the path slowly. Fatigue etched their stern faces. They dispersed quickly, each searching out his own family.

Abigail called, "Tom, over here."

Caleb ran to take Tom's gun and knapsack, his many questions stilled by the look on his father's face.

"What is it?" Abigail embraced her husband.

He held her tightly and led them to a bench, "Sit down." he said.

Abigail held onto his hand.

He turned to Caleb. "Ye too."

They sat. Tom stood in front of them. One hand held Abigail's tightly, the other rested on Caleb's shoulder.

"We followed the soldiers to the Indian fence. We saw no signs of Indians, nor did we hear any drumming. " 'Twas so quiet, it could have been a normal trip to the village, except for our soldiers' clinking armor.

"Then we saw it." A sob rushed from his throat. He swallowed. "On poles ahead of us," he groaned, "The six people from Bourne garrison that were killed..." He took a deep breath. "The Wampanoags had cut off their heads and their hands and stuck them on poles in the path."

Abigail gasped and grew pale. Caleb choked.

Tom squeezed Caleb's shoulder. Caleb winced.

"Will and his father's heads...."

Caleb heard no more. Retching and gagging, he turned and ran toward the open fields beyond the house. The copper pendant banged on his breastbone. He tugged it over his head and, swinging it by its thong, flung it away and ran blindly into the woods.

"Caleb!" Abigail rose and called after him.

"Let him go. The Indians have left Mount Hope." Tom put his arms around Abigail, holding her close. His chin rested on the top of her head. Abigail wept. Tom patted her shoulders. His eyes clouded with tears. He bit his lip, forcing himself to hold back the anguish he felt.

Without a word the two of them turned slowly. Hand in hand, they too walked the path Caleb had taken.

XXXI
NARRAGANSETT SAFETY

Ontaquos lay perfectly still in the hot summer thicket. His hand clamped over his little brother's shoulder firmly, warning him not to make a sound. Shannuke's head pressed into the dark, dry earth. The smell of the soil was rich under summer grasses and reeds. Without a sound, Shannuke brought his hand to his face. He pinched his nose, covered his mouth, and squelched a sneeze. His shoulders shook in silent laughter. Ontaquos' fingers played a noiseless staccato of understanding on his brother's back. They waited silently.

Several feet from where they lay, Awuanaguss soldiers marched along the trail. Ontaquos and Shannuke heard them muttering and slapping at the black flies. The two brothers and all the other Wampanoags held their breath. No one made a sound. Mothers cupped their hands over infant's noses and mouths to silence them. The tall reeds swayed over them.

Buzzing flies were repelled by the odor of cedar and sweetgrass rubbed into their glistening bodies. Finally the sound of clanking armor and cursing men slowly faded. No one moved.

Ontaquos slithered through the reeds and disappeared. He crawled toward the path. Finally standing on the trail, he imitated a bird sound, "Whippoorwill! Whippoorwill!", signaling that it was safe to come out.

The hidden people rose from the thickets and joined Ontaquos. Everyone smiled and discussed their safe hiding place softly, but fear remained in their eyes.

Ontaquos held his hand for silence. "We are not far from the Narragansetts. By the time Moon Woman tells Sun God to pull his light out of the sky, we'll be at the village. We can make good time now that the Longknives have gone. Let's get started. We'll soon be safe."

Everyone hoisted his belongings up on his back and followed the young Warrior. Little Shannuke strained under his heavy load. Ottucke nodded and smiled encouragement as she bent forward under the weight of her household mats and family belongings.

Ontaquos paused to help his grandmother with her burden. He helped her up from her sitting position and adjusted the bundle on her back. She stumbled but righted herself quickly, rubbed her bones where the bundle chafed, and stepped onto the trail. Pequawas followed her, shuffling along with dragging footsteps. His breathing was labored, but pride and determination glowed in his aged eyes and he kept pace with the tribe.

Sun God slanted his late rays onto the path. The solid ground of the forest became soft and squishy. Ontaquos led the way into the monstrous swamp. Muck and water oozed from the ground making walking difficult. Snakes slithered along the wetness. Frogs croaked at the intruders. At last Ontaquos held up his hand and cautioned his people to stop. Ahead of them in the thickening dusk stood a huge palisade fence.

"Ooowww!" Ontaquos' wolf howl soared to the sky above.

An answer came immediately. Soon after the response, Ontaquos watched a young man step into the clearing where they waited. His hair hung in long black braids. He wore no war paint. The soft flaps of his deerskin breechclout slapped his thighs and the backs of his legs as he walked.

"Netop." He licked his forearm in greeting.

Ontaquos was startled to hear a Narragansett accent. "Netop," he replied.

The Narragansett looked surprised. All the Wampanoags smiled and said 'Netop' with the Narragansett accent. They all laughed together. The young Narragansett chuckled and led them onto a secret path that took them into the safety of the village. Ontaquos gasped at the size. Dozens of longhouses sprawled out, stretching beyond his view in the deep dusk. Wigwams nestled between the longhouses. The thickening gloom outlined hundreds of people. It was the largest village he'd ever seen.

As torches and campfires burst through the darkness, Ontaquos saw hundreds of Warriors lounging about, visiting, smoking, mending weapons, and relaxing. Some of them played the peach pit game. Women prepared food, made mats from piles of fibers, played with their children, and gathered in groups to visit. Children ran and played everywhere. Ontaquos relaxed. It was good to be inside.

His Narragansett guide turned to him. "What is the news?"

Ontaquos told of their attack on Swanzey and then of their escape by boats and rafts from their own village at Mauntop, and how they'd floated across the bay in darkness to unite with Weetamo, Queen leader of the Pocassets, who was waiting to join the war.

"Can you imagine the look on the Longknives' faces when they got to the camp and found only a few dogs wandering around?" Ontaquos laughed. "They were so stupid, they built a fort at the entrance to our lands to seal us up. It took so long to build, we ferried all our people and all our supplies right out from under them.

"Now, we've divided into groups. Our Warriors and Weetemo's have gone to join the Nipmucs in the interior, and I've brought the women, children, and old people here with you."

The Narragansett nodded. "If they're such foolish fighters, it won't take you long to drive them out."

"Tell me, why don't you Narragansetts join us?"

"Our sachems deal with the Awuanaguss who call themselves Bay people and live in their place 'Boston', not the Awuanaguss from the place they call Plimoth. We agreed to keep the peace and let you and your allies fight. The Longknives are such stupid fighters, it won't be long before you've won. In the meantime, we're able to keep your women and children and elders safe here in our fortress. There's no way anyone can ever get in here."

"That's true." Ontaquos turned. "Come, meet my family."

"And eat some succotash too?"

Ontaquos rubbed his empty stomach, "Of course, NEETOP."

They both laughed and went toward the cooking pots.

The warm breeze gently rippled the blackness of the rustling leaves. Fireflies glowed in the dark. Ontaquos smiled. It was good to be safe among friends.

XXXII
PREPARING FOR WAR

The bitter winter cold crept through the cracks in the wooden clapboards, forcing drafts of frigid air into the room. The fires in the open fireplace glowed red and blue with cooking coals. Abigail's face flushed with the heat. She pulled one cast iron pot to the front of the hearth and pushed another toward the center. Outside, she heard boots stomping snow. She straightened, turning quickly. She watched him step into the room shaking snow from his heavy coat. He crossed the room and hung it on a peg next to the fire. He turned to the open hearth rubbing his hands together and spreading them toward the blue coals. Turning his backside to the fire, he rubbed his britches, reveling in the warmth.

Abigail faced him, her gaze level with his chin. He'd grown since summer. The boy was gone. Now he had the lean look of a man. His jaw was angular with the beginnings of a blonde beard. His eyebrows had thickened and his vivid blue eyes had recessed deeper into their sockets. She handed him a bowl of stew and Caleb sat next to the fire eating hungrily.

Tom stepped through the door with Lad, who padded over to Caleb, sniffing at his bowl. "The militia's down the road. They'll be here soon," Tom said.

Caleb patted Abigail's shoulder. "Don't look so worried, Mother. I'll be back before ye know I've gone, and with a string of scalps to prove I've done my share." He gave her his bowl and stood up.

"Be careful, son." Tom handed him his flintlock.

"I will," Caleb said. "And ye too."

"Don't worry. We'll be fine." Tom smiled at Abigail.

Abigail helped Caleb with his coat, wrapped a scarf around his neck, and handed him his hat and mittens. Tom gave Caleb his knapsack, powder horn, and bullet pouch. Caleb took them and embraced Abigail.

"God be with ye," she spoke softly.

"And ye and father too." He turned and flicked up the latch.

"Wait." She rummaged through her sewing basket and held something toward him. It glowed, reflecting the flame from the fire. "Here." She handed it to him.

He reached for it, holding it by its thong. The glint from it reflected in his eyes mixing flecks of copper with bright blue.

"I found it after ye'd left that day." She paused, "I kept it thinking ye might want it to remind ye of...." Her voice trailed off.

He frowned, looked from her to the pendant, then closed his fingers around it and stuffed it in his knapsack. "Thank ye. 'Twill remind me of many things."

"I thought 'twould."

Outside, the clank of armor rattled against the winter silence. Inside, they heard horses neighing and snorting impatiently. There was a knock on the door. Abigail opened it.

The sergeant stood outside. "The militia be ready to go."

Caleb nodded to the man and kissed his mother. "I'll be back," he whispered. He shut the door and stepped into the winter cold. He adjusted his knapsack and shouldered his gun. "Where be we going?"

"Smith's Trading House in the Rhode Island Colony. We be joining troops from

Plimoth, The Bay, and Connecticut."

"Isn't that Narragansett Indian territory?"

"Aye. Let's get going."

Caleb nodded to his neighbors. He counted twenty Swanzey men. He fell into line and trudged along the familiar trail into town. Passing the lane to Will's house was always painful.

At the wharf where boats were waiting, Caleb's group joined others and soon the boats were loaded and ready to go. Caleb huddled under the rail with the other men. Their bodies were packed tightly together and the warmth kept him from freezing.

The winter sky darkened and sleet pelted them, soaking into woolen coats and numbing them. He closed his eyes and let his body sway with the motion of the boat. Finally he dozed. The bow scraping the shore woke him and he grabbed the rail and tried to rise. His muscles were so cramped, he couldn't move. Someone gave him a push and he straightened up.

"Come on, Caleb. We're here." Noah Wilson helped him out of the boat. Caleb grabbed his knapsack, gun, and bullet pouch and wearily followed Noah and the others.

XXXIII
REPORTING THE MARCH

The sky reminded Ontaquos of clay cookpots that hung over the firepits in the winter longhouses. The heavy grey clouds seemed almost black. They puffed like stuffed squirrels' cheeks and would spit out snow before the day was over. Ontaquos would have liked a squirrel. Hunting had been terrible.

Suddenly his neck prickled. He sensed their presence before he heard clanking metal and snorting horses. He brushed away his footprints and leapt from the frozen trail, crawling into a hollow log. He pulled dead leaves and brush on top of himself. Rotten wood dust filled his eyes. He blinked, and rubbed them clear, then peeked out through the dry, dead branches. He heard creaking wagon wheels and whinnying horses and the endless tramping of plodding feet pounding in the winter stillness.

He saw them. Mohegan Indian scouts wearing bright blue blankets and carrying English flintlocks led the way. He hated those traitors. They prayed to the English "Lord Jesus" and fought with the Longknives against the Wampanoag and the Nipmuc. As they approached his hiding place, he barely breathed. His body ached in its cramped position. His muscles knotted in spasms, but he dared not move.

After the scouts, came officers on horseback followed by hundreds of marchers all carrying weapons and hunched against the cold. They wore warm scarves around their faces. Ontaquos watched silently. Finally, the long column disappeared around the bend of the trail that led to Smith's garrison and trading house.

He waited until darkness began to obscure the path and there were no signs of scouts and stragglers. In the still forest, he stretched inside the log. Wood dust enveloped him. He blinked. His feet and hands were numb. He wiggled them and felt the throbbing pain of returning blood. He kept them moving until the pain left. He poked his head into the darkening day and dragged himself out of his hiding place. He ran for the village.

Ontaquos felt his way in the wintery

darkness. He sensed the palisade fence much as a blind man feels a solid force in his path. He groped along the outer edge of the huge posts and felt the secret opening. He went straight to the Council House. He stepped inside. Cattail torches mounted on the walls cast eerie shadows on the mats lining the interior. Canonchet sat cross-legged on his fur-strewn sleeping pallet surrounded by his advisors and Warrior leaders. One of Canonchet's hands plucked the coarse, rough bear fur under him. His other hand cradled his stone pipe. He was staring at the carved mountain lion curled around the tobacco bowl. Its sightless eyes stared back. The Narragansett leader shifted his gaze and with an almost imperceptible nod motioned Ontaquos to sit.

Ontaquos crawled onto the platform near the door. Beaver fur tickled the inside of his bare thighs between his leggings and breechclout. He let his warm deer cloak slide down his naked back and lump into a pillow behind him. He crossed his legs, leaned his elbows on his knees, and cupped his chin in his hands. His black eyes glistened. He waited.

Canonchet turned to his Medicine Man. "What news do you think our young Wampanoag Warrior brings us?"

"He has something of great importance to tell us. I see it in his twitching muscles and tightened jaw."

Canonchet commanded, "Speak, Wampanoag Warrior.

The elders leaned forward to hear Ontaquos' report. When he finished, the Sachem turned to the others. "They can't be coming here. We have signed a peace agreement that we won't fight."

"But we do have Wampanoag women, children and old ones. And guards like this one who has just spoken." said one of them nodding toward Ontaquos.

Another Council member spoke, "We did agree to turn all Wampanoags in to the Longknives and even send their heads to Plimoth if any of Metacom's people appeared here."

The Council members winked at each other at the absurdity of the English request.

"No one can trust the lying English anyway. They cheat us out of our lands and throw us in their jails whenever they want."

"They make marks on their paper and have us make marks and then change our words and say that it is so when it is not."

Canonchet held his hand for silence. "I don't think the Longknives will try to come here, but if they do, they'll never get in. Our fortress is too strong and they don't know the secret path. We'll prepare our Warriors just in case, but I don't think they'll be so foolish." He turned to Ontaquos and smiled. "You've done well. No matter what happens, we'll be ready."

Ontaquos smiled, grabbed his cloak, and walked to the doorway. He was glad his family was safe deep in this Narragansett fortress.

XXXIV
THE HARD PART

Caleb dragged his feet over the frozen ground. Big white snowflakes trickled slowly onto his heavy coat. The winter sky darkened. His shoulders ached. His gun barrel pressed into the back of his neck. One arm hung over the gunstock. He alternated tucking his hands inside his woolen coat and felt the tingling blood slowly pulsing to his fingertips. His aching fingers grasped the copper amulet he'd put around his neck. He rubbed it often. It radiated warmth from his body and felt good to hold. He thought of his 'netop', and wondered where he was. It was difficult to think of him as the enemy.

His legs felt sluggish and heavy, and he stumbled over the slippery ground, bumping against his companions. Over one thousand men had been traveling for several hours. Caleb's sergeant had passed the word. They'd eat while marching. Caleb munched on his journey cake, thinking of his mother's warm hearth and hot food.

The long column followed its Indian

guide into the deep swamp. Men slipped frequently on the uneven terrain. Caleb fell twice on icy patches of frozen swamp water. He muttered, "I never thought soldiering 'twould be like this."

"This is the easy part." Noah Wilson's face hardened.

Caleb looked at him sideways. "What's the hardest part?"

"Ye'll find out."

Caleb felt the heavy lump of dough in his stomach. His mouth was dry. He shivered. Suddenly in the distance, he heard the sounds of battle. As they came closer, the noise was deafening. Bullets whistled. Guns cracked. Men shouted. Some screamed. Indians screeched tauntingly from behind a huge palisade fence. Caleb saw soldiers in another company tugging at huge Great Danes with spiked collars. The dogs bayed and strained to enter the fort.

The palisade fence seemed impenetrable. Suddenly Caleb saw soldiers clamber onto a tree that had been hastily placed in a section where the fence was not finished. Murderous cross fire chopped many of them down. Caleb watched scores of English soldiers crawl into the entrance. Others tried scaling the wall in spite of the deadly barrage of bullets. Inside, Warriors waited with guns and lethal tomahawks. The ground between the forest and palisade fence was littered with dead and wounded English soldiers.

Caleb's mouth dried with fear. He clutched his gun. A short axe hung from his belt. He brushed it quickly to make sure it was easily accessible. He followed his group. They pushed themselves across the huge log and tumbled inside.

Noah tapped Caleb's shoulder. "Follow me and stay close."

Caleb stared at the dozens of longhouses. He heard sounds of frightened women and children wailing inside the dwellings. Men fought everywhere. English clothing and metal breast plates mingled with Indian fur clad or naked glistening torsos decorated in garish colors and designs.

Caleb turned to follow Noah but was pushed into a corner by a snarling Great Dane wrestling with a writhing, twisting Indian. Caleb aimed his gun. The struggling form squirmed out of range. The Indian twisted around and smashed his tomahawk into the huge beast's skull. The dog's jaws slackened as its body went limp in death. The wounded Indian leapt from the dead dog and charged Caleb. Caleb squeezed his trigger. The gun jammed. Caleb spun out of the way. His copper amulet swung around his neck, twirling in the air. He grabbed his axe and turned to grapple with his foe. Their bodies collided. They wrestled, each with his axe ready to kill. Backing up, Caleb stumbled over the dead dog and fell. His enemy charged forward, tomahawk raised. Caleb threw his arm up to ward off the blow. His other hand groped frantically for his axe. He found it, and swinging wildly, he desperately lunged forward, smashing it into his attacker's skull. Blood spurted from the lethal wound and splattered Caleb's face and body. He sidestepped the careening body and watched it fall. He felt like an observer hovering above. This seemed to be happening to someone else.

Caleb stared at the dead Warrior. Under the blood and garish paint was a young face maybe Will's age. Caleb tried to recall Will. He couldn't. He gagged and vomited. Then he slowly wiped his bloody hands on his leather britches.

Noah came running toward him. He stopped, looked at the dead Warrior, and clasped Caleb's shoulder. "Now ye know the hard part," he said quietly. Turning, he shouted, "Come on. 'Tis not over yet."

Caleb followed Noah and the others, firing his gun or swinging his axe to attack the enemy. They fought their way deeper into the village, slowly pushing the outnumbered warriors out of the compound. Ahead of Caleb and Noah, the advancing soldiers paused long enough to ignite some of the longhouses. Hundreds of Indians swarmed out of the burning buildings. Soldiers shot at them as they emerged.

Caleb stood horrified at the slaughter. He saw a soldier laugh, pointing to a young girl engulfed in flames. Caleb loaded his gun, aimed, and shot her in the heart. She stopped shrieking. He stood numbly watching snow cover her burned body. A deep sob rushed from his throat and he screamed his outrage at all he had seen and done that day.

XXXV
ATTACKED ALONE

In the late afternoon, the mixture of snow and smoke from the burning longhouses made it impossible to see. Caleb's sergeant sent him to look for wounded English soldiers to bring back to the empty Indian dwellings.

Lumps covered with snow lay everywhere indicating bodies lying in the white stillness. Puddles of blood oozed and congealed in the whiteness. Caleb brushed the snow away and turned over a dead Indian. His vivid memory of his first killing leapt into his mind and he gagged at the recollection. He gently pushed the snow back over the Indian's body.

Finding no wounded English survivors nor bodies of dead Englishmen to return to the shelter, Caleb returned to his platoon and began helping with the wounded that had been gathered.

"We be returning to Smith's Trading House," his sergeant said, loading a groaning, bloody man onto a litter. "Give me a hand with this one." He motioned to a lump so covered with snow Caleb hadn't realized it was a man. The sergeant grabbed the man's armpits and Caleb hoisted his legs.

Brushing snow from his face, Caleb recognized him. "Don't worry, Andrew, we'll get ye safely home."

"God willing," murmured the Swanzey man.

Caleb went to retrieve poles from one of the few standing dwellings. "Why don't we use these longhouses and get the wounded out of the snow and into shelter?" he asked Noah, who had joined him.

"We've got orders to return to Smith's garrison."

"In this storm?" Caleb peered into the blackness. The trail out of the village was obliterated.

"They be afraid we'll be attacked by the Narragansetts and the Wampanoags if we stay here," said Noah, cutting wigwam poles away from their frames.

Caleb trimmed a pole and handed it to Noah, who was making a sled to drag the wounded. He sighed thinking of the tortuous journey in store for them.

The sergeant appeared. "We've got them all. We'll bury our dead when we get to Smith's. Let's start back."

Caleb fell in line.

"Not ye. We've been ordered to burn all remaining dwellings. Ye stay here and be sure this one is fired. It shouldn't take long. Then join us if ye can, otherwise follow the trail and we'll see ye back at the garrison." The sergeant started moving toward the trail.

Noah yelled at Caleb as he left, dragging a litter. "Keep yer eyes peeled. I'll watch for ye and come back to help ye if I can."

Caleb nodded. "Thank ye, Noah. I won't be long. God go with ye." He waved and watched the men retreat into darkness.

Standing alone in the gloom, Caleb held a handful of tinder and struck a spark with his flint against his metal knife. He cupped his hand protectively against snow and wind and added more tinder to the tiny flame. Igniting a dried branch with the starter fire, he touched it to the bark slab covering the longhouse and watched the flames eat into the night blackness. The heat seared his eyebrows. He stepped back quickly.

Suddenly a form hurtled out of the

darkness and smashed him to the ground,
knocking his breath out of his lungs. The
flames from the burning building illuminated
the gruesomely painted face staring into his.
Caleb struggled, but the Indian straddled
him, using his knees to pin Caleb's arms to
the snowy ground. The Indian grabbed
Caleb's hair, forcing his head back. The
pendant fell out of Caleb's collar and
reflected the bright firelight.

The Indian stared. He lowered his
tomahawk, grasped the metal disc and peered
into Caleb's face. "Netop?" Ontaquos
hesitated, then slowly released his grip. He
got up and hauled Caleb to his feet. The two
stared at each other. Ontaquos fingered the
pendant. He smiled. So did Caleb.
Ontaquos pointed toward the Englishmen's
trail. He motioned Caleb to go. He raised
his hand in salute and called, "Netop."

"Goodbye, Netop," Caleb called. He
retrieved his knapsack, and weapons and
trudged toward the trail. Ontaquos watched
him go. Then he too disappeared silently
into the swirling snowstorm. Trembling,
Caleb followed the trail left by his returning
army. His mind, full of the day's event,

pictured Will's face clearly. It mingled with the burned girl's face, the dead warrior's face and his Wampanoag friend's face.

"Netop," they all said, over and over.

XXXVI
DEATH AND LIFE

The late spring rain felt good on Ontaquos' body. He lay behind a haystack outside a garrison several miles from an Awuanaguss town in the Nipmuc country far from his familiar coastal village of Mauntop. He loaded his gun and followed his father. Running swiftly from a haystack to an abandoned cart in the open farmyard, they joined several warriors who prepared flaming arrows to burn the settlers out. The garrison's thatched roof smoldered where earlier shafts had landed. The heavy rain deluge of moments before had snuffed out the burning torches of the attack. This siege was like so many others that Ontaquos had known since the fierce winter fight in the Narragansett swamp so long ago. Ontaquos watched several Nipmucs and Wampanoags charge the front of the house. They were shot trying to chop through the main door with their tomahawks. The Nipmucs and their allies gathered their wounded, and retreated, returning to where Ontqaquos and the others were waiting. They all decided to wait for Sun God to leave the sky.

Huddling beneath the wagon, Ontaquos waited. Darkness finally came.

"Get some sleep." Kuttiomp patted his son's shoulder. "There are enough of us here to take turns watching. The Longknives cannot escape. We'll burn them out in the morning."

Ontaquos and Kuttiomp crawled back to the haystack. Ontaquos curled up in the hay. He was soon dreaming of long hungry marches and cold miserable months of attacking, killing, and fleeing. The pursuing English soldiers seemed to be everywhere. His own yelling woke him and he sucked in a deep breath of the mild spring night air.

Kuttiomp spoke softly. "The dreaming is with all of us. It has not been easy, especially the hunger, but we are driving the English out of the Valley-of-the-Long-River here in the Nipmuc country."

"I know." Ontaquos was wide awake now. "But this land is so different from home. I miss the sea."

"It won't be much longer. When we've forced the Longknives out of these hills, we'll return home and drive the rest of them into the sea."

"I hope so." Ontaquos stood and stretched in the moonlight. He looked down at his father. "Why don't you sleep and I'll stand guard. I can't sleep anyway."

Kuttiomp rolled himself into a patch of hay and soon snored gently. Ontaquos stared at the quiet house outlined in a moonbeam and wondered what the English would do. They couldn't escape. In the morning, warriors would burn the building. They would capture or kill the English as soon as they burst out of the building.

Ontaquos rubbed his scarred bicep. His fingers probed the thick ridges of the first scar. He remembered his best friend, the first one to fall so long ago. Then he fingered the other scars. These two slashes below the first were for his grandparents who had burned in the Narragansett Winter Village, the place he'd thought was so safe. His mother had told him how it'd happened when the family reunited in the first Nipmuc camp. She told how she'd tried to help Pequawas and Nitka out of the burning Narragansett longhouse. His grandparents had clung to each other tightly and stepped out of the way to let the younger, stronger ones escape. Ottucke had screamed her agony as they'd pushed her out the door with Shannuke just before the flaming rafters fell.

Ontaquos recalled his weeks and months of hunger and fear. Moving from one temporary camp to another, he'd been in many battles. He'd killed more Awuanaguss than he could count on his hands. Now he was tired. He wanted to go home to the sea. As Moon Woman slowly walked into the night sky, he started to doze. She sent a moon beam down, brushing her light across his face. He roused himself, smiled up at her, and stood guard.

Much later, Sun God tiptoed into the morning sky, nodding at Moon Woman, who stood boldly watching his arrival. She nodded at him as she watched Sun God outline the house. Ontaquos shook his father's shoulder. It was time.

Soon flaming arrows fired the roof. Behind Ontaquos, a warrior screamed a battle cry. A few of them rolled a burning wagon down the hill. It rammed the house and ignited wooden clapboards. The house was engulfed in fire. People poured out into the courtyard. Ontaquos watched a Warrior grab an older woman who had knelt by a wounded Englishman trying to staunch the blood oozing from his chest. The Nipmuc seized the woman's hair and drove his tomahawk into her scalp. She fell motionless, blood streaming from her head.

Finally it was over. Ontaquos and his father stood looking at the dead bodies. In the silence, Ontaquos heard a whimper. He searched. At the rear of the dwelling, he found a small child hiding under an overturned water barrel. Ontaquos lifted the frightened toddler and held her close. She screamed. Ontaquos tried to soothe her. She sobbed quietly in his arms. He held her and returned to the warriors. One of the Nipmucs tried to snatch the child, raising his tomahawk. Ontaquos and Kuttiomp warned him away.

"What will you do with this one?" asked Kuttiomp, stroking the child's golden hair.

"There's been enough killing here today. This little one will live. I shall take her to Ottucke."

"She will be pleased," answered his father.

Ontaquos cradled the little girl in his arms and trotted along the path to camp.

XXXVII
GOING HOME

Several hours later, Ontaquos and Kuttiomp arrived at the clearing near their temporary wigwam. Ottucke looked up. Her quick smile softened the deep lines in her thin face. Her deep brown eyes reflected her joy and relief at their safe return when she saw them walking slowly toward her.

She rose quickly to greet them, embracing them both with a hug, then reached to unfold the deerskin blanket to see what Ontaquos carried in the bundle in his arms. He handed her the sleeping child, and watched her tenderly arrange the child on a soft fur. As she lightly touched the soft golden hair, and inspected the youngster, Ontaquos told Ottucke how he'd found her, and then sank wearily onto a mat, rolled it around himself, and slept. This time he was too tired to dream.

It was late afternoon when he awoke. His stomach ached. He went to the cooking pot. His mother knelt at the firepit grinding a handful of acorns she'd found in a squirrel's nest. She added them to the simmering water in the clay pot. Ontaquos dipped in and scooped out a spoonful of broth. It was thin and runny like the ones he'd made when he'd wintered alone, not like the stews they had in the winter village. He saw the sadness in Ottucke's thin face as she watched him finish the sparse meal and wipe his hands on his worn breechclout.

He smiled at her, "Don't worry, Mother. We'll get back home and you'll have your garden again."

She nodded and rose to comfort the crying child, who had awakened. She held her close, singing to her, and soothing her as she fed her the thin soup.

Ontaquos walked away and stood gazing at the rows of soft, blue, rolling hills reaching across the land as far as he could see. Leaves on the oaks were the size of field mice ears. Soft greens and pinks of new growth colored the shrubs and wild plants dotting this Nipmuc countryside. He did so miss the cries of seagulls whirling and circling, lifted on the hands of the unseen Wind Gods.

It was corn planting season. If he'd been home, Ottuke would have cleared her fields.

She'd have dropped kernels into the small mounds of earth, then added bean seeds so the vines could crawl up the cornstalks and finally she would have planted squash all around the base to help keep the weeds away. There would have been feasting and games and new clothes and everyone would have joined in celebrating Earth Mother's return from the cave of the Ice Spirit. He loved the excitement of the return to their summer village on the bay.

He turned away from the view and returned to the clearing. He flung himself on the ground and stretched out on his soft cedar mats. He stared at the blue sky and closed his eyes against the glare of the spring sun. A shadow crossed his face and he opened his eyes to see what had caused it.

His father stood over him. "Come. Metacom has called for all warriors to gather at his wigwam."

Ontaquos leapt up.

Metacom stood consulting with his advisors. Kuttiomp went to join them. Ontaquos stood with the warriors, watching and waiting. No one said anything.

Finally, Metacom nodded to his council

and faced the waiting warriors. His face was thin and strained but his expression strong and determined. Blood ran from a gash on his left arm. "We shall speak no more of our brother who leads the Narragansett people."

Ontaquos pictured Conanchet, then blocked his name from his thoughts. He and the others wondered what had happened.

Metacom continued, "A messenger just brought the news. He was captured by the Longknives who turned him over to their allies, the Mohegans-who-would-not-join-us. It was they, our hated enemy, who killed him." He sighed wearily. "So many of our brothers have gone to the spirit world of Kiehtan.

"It is time for us to return to the land of our birth. There we shall gain new strength and I will lead our people to victory just as we have helped the Nipmuc drive the English from their territory.

"Our brothers to the north have said they would join us in our fight if we gave them time to prepare. I shall send messengers to see if they are ready. Come. Let us prepare to go home."

Kuttiomp turned to follow Metacom, but

before leaving, he spoke to Ontaquos. "You'll be one of the guards. Be sure to watch for stragglers. We'll travel by night and rest at Sun God's coming."

Ontaquos nodded. He hurried to check the outlying areas and trotted silently through the woods. He heard the sounds of his people preparing to break camp and follow the warriors along the trail that led out of the Nipmuc country.

There would be many times for Sun God to come and go before they'd be back to the bays and hills of home, but he was happy. They were going home.

XXXVIII
KING PHILIP'S RETURN

Caleb rested his gun against the fence. He chopped into the earth with his hoe, biting into the weeds, exposing them to the air and death. He was one of several Swanzey men assigned to the cornfields. Guards stood near the woods. He worked quickly among the rows of cornstalks choked by the rampant weeds, pausing occasionally to wipe sweat from his eyes with a swipe of his forearm. He heard galloping hooves, dropped his hoe and ran to grab his gun. The guards aimed at the sound. Emerging from the shadows of the thick forest, a messenger came into view. Everyone rushed toward him to hear his news.

He shouted, "King Philip's been seen not twenty miles from here. He and his people are returning home. Everyone is to go to Myles' garrison." The messenger dug his heels into his horse and galloped off.

Caleb ran for home, his hoe in one hand, his flintlock in the other.

"Mother! Father! King Philip is

returning to Mount Hope. His urgent tone brought his parents from their chores. He told them what he'd heard from the messenger. Gathering their belongings, and herding their animals ahead of them, they were soon on their way to the safety of the garrison. It had become a familiar routine for them. There were far fewer families now. Many had abandoned their homes and sailed across the bay to the Island safety of Newport where Quakers had taken the refugees in. Many others had been killed during the long year of bloody warfare.

Abigail had refused to leave her home and had insisted they return to it each time the Indians left the territory. Now they were staying at the garrison once again. The families settled into the familiar routine of garrison living. Women worked together preparing meals and assigning sleeping areas. Men arranged for sentry duty and care for the animals.

Two days later, Caleb stood with a group of volunteers preparing to join troops from Plimoth. He stood outside with the others, listening to his sergeant. "This time we'll finish it. If we can kill or capture King

Philip, the war'll be over. We'll join the Plimoth soldiers at the mouth of the river."

Abigail handed Caleb his knapsack. "Be careful."

"Don't worry, Mother. I'll be fine." He rubbed his pendant.

Tom left the group of garrison guards. His hair had greyed considerably in the last year. The lines on his face were deeply etched. He stood facing his son. "God be with ye." He squeezed Caleb's shoulder.

The sergeant mounted his horse. "Let's be off." He wheeled his mount onto the trail and the small band of volunteers followed behind.

At the bend of the trail, Caleb turned and waved. Abigail flicked her apron and Tom raised his arm in farewell. Caleb and the others entered the forest. No one said anything. They emerged into clear open marshland several hours later. In the distance, they heard supply carts bumping over the main path to the river. They finally joined the milling throng of men from Plimoth.

"Wait here." The sergeant went to report to the officer in charge. Caleb sat down under the shade of a huge oak. His companions sprawled around him. He missed Noah, who'd been wounded on an earlier patrol and was recovering at the garrison.

A young man, younger than Caleb, walked over to the Swanzey group. He stood in front of Caleb, staring at him. "My name be Joshua. I hail from Plimoth. Where'd ye get the pendant?"

Caleb stuffed the pendant into his shirtfront. " 'Twas given to me by a 'netop'."

"Ye have a heathen friend? Is he a loyal Indian?"

"No. He fights with King Philip."

The incredulous look on Joshua's face made Caleb laugh, and he told him about the wildcat, and the injured cow, and the winter battle in the Narragansett Great Swamp.

Joshua sat quietly after Caleb had finished. "I never thought of them as people."

"Aye, 'tis sad. Most don't." Caleb stretched out on the ground, resting his head on his knapsack.

Joshua flicked his tongue against his dry lips. "I wonder when we'll fight."

Caleb looked at him with sympathy. He remembered how he'd been at the Swamp Fight. "We'll have to find them first." He saw the look of concern on Joshua's face. "Don't worry. Ye'll be so busy ye won't have a chance to be scared," he lied. "Rest while ye can." Caleb closed his eyes against the summer brightness and was soon asleep.

XXXIX
WAMPANOAG TREASON

Ontaquos breathed in the familiar smells of seaweed, salt water, and forest. It was good to be home. Standing guard high on the rocky mount, he gazed out across the sunlit bays and rivers. He heard a noise and turned quickly. His replacement stepped onto the ledge.

Ontaquos gathered up his gun, powder horn, and bullet pouch. "I've seen nothing unusual. From this spot you can detect any movement. Only the secret trail is difficult to observe."

"It's a safe place to be. Metacom chose wisely. Rest well. No one will surprise our people. I shall search with the eye of a hawk." The sentry shaded his eyes and looked across the bay to Swanzey.

Ontaquos smiled and crawled down the ledge to the camp below. Entering the village, he heard loud voices. He went to see who was quarreling. Two brothers stood glaring angrily at one another. Metacom and

Kuttiomp approached from the opposite side. Ontaquos watched.

Metacom confronted the brothers. "Why are my warriors arguing?"

The older brother spoke. "Longknife soldiers are heading for our homeland. They're being led by Captain Benjamin Church. He knows our ways. He has loyal Indian scouts who teach him our secrets. I feel all is lost. We must surrender to this Benjamin Church to save our women and children. Even now all over the countryside our brothers are turning themselves in as the Awuanaguss gain strength and destroy our allies."

"We argue because I say we must continue to fight," interrupted the younger brother.

Metacom answered, "You are right." Turning to the older man he said, "When have you learned more than your leader? I have consulted with the wise men of the tribe. We were given the sign of victory last corn planting when our first warrior died."

Ontaquos recoiled at the painful memory of his friend's death.

"You speak of treason and the unthinkable," Metacom continued. "We will rally our people once again from these sacred grounds and with new allies, we will rise and drive the Awuanaguss into the sea."

The older brother replied, "There've been many of our allies who've given themselves to the Longknives. Others have released their Awuanaguss prisoners and have renounced your war and joined the English cause."

Metacom interrupted, "What you say is true, but many more remain loyal to me and I would expect you to be one of them."

"I feel our cause is lost. There's been too much suffering. I've heard the Longknives won't kill us if we surrender."

Metacom pulled his pistol from his belt. He aimed at the older brother. "I order you to pledge your loyalty to me and our cause."

The warrior stood firm. "I implore you to surrender."

Metacom pulled the trigger. The bullet struck the warrior's chest. He slumped forward and slowly slid to the ground. A gurgling sound came from his mouth. Then he lay silent.

The younger brother cradled his dead brother. He grasped his knife with his free hand and slashed his own arm. His blood mingled with his brother's. He wept.

Metacom turned and strode toward his wigwam. Kuttiomp guided his son to a tall pine away from the campsite and the mourning man. He put his arm around his son and spoke softly. "You have done well and I'm proud of you. You are young and have much to learn. I don't know what will happen to any of us. It may be as Metacom predicts. It could be we are doomed as the dead one said. My place is with Metacom and I will remain to the end.

"I want you to fight, but above all you must protect your mother, Shannuke, and the other women and children. You must lead them to safety as you did once before. It is you and the young ones who are the future of our people. Take as many as you can to the North People. They will take you in." He turned to leave. "I'm proud of you. I love you very much."

Ontaquos' throat choked with a huge lump. He finally managed to say, "I shall do as you ask." His eyes searched his father's face, and he said, " And I love you."

That night, no one saw the dead warrior's younger brother slip onto the secret trail that led from the mount.

XL
METACOM

Caleb felt someone shake him gently. He leapt from the ground. It was dark, but moonlight outlined the figure standing in front of him.

His sergeant spoke, "Be quiet. We be going after King Philip. One of his warriors will lead us right into his camp. They say the Injun's angry 'cus King Philip killed his brother. Captain Benjamin Church will be leading us. Come, we be leaving now."

Caleb grabbed his equipment and followed his group. A shiver of excitement rippled along his neck. Slowly, silently, he and the other soldiers crept along the path. Caleb was impressed. No one could have come by boat. They would have been discovered long before they could land. The secret path was well hidden. No one would have found it without a guide.

The order was whispered along the line to halt. Caleb stood on the path looking across the bay to Swanzey.

His sergeant approached him. "We be
about a mile from the camp. The trail turns
away from the water and heads along the
center of the mount. Ye stay here where the
path branches off and guard it. We don't
want heathens getting away."

Caleb nodded and crouched in a crevice.
He rested.

******

Ontaquos started up from his sleeping
mats. Gunfire had shattered the stillness of
the summer night. Then he heard
Longknives shouting to one another in the
darkness. He rushed to Ottucke, who was
clutching the screaming blonde toddler. He
roused Shannuke, propelling them all into
the safety of the swamp away from the camp.
Returning to the clearing, he scooped up
other children and herded them and their
mothers away from the firing lines to his
family's hiding place. Soon he'd gathered
several dozen mothers with their children.
They huddled in silence together.

It was impossible to see what was
happening. Ontaquos heard men running
and shouting. Guns roared. From out of the

dark, he heard Metacom's voice rallying his warriors as he ran from his shelter to the fierce battle below. Ontaquos sensed Metacom's form racing past them down the side of a hill to attack the enemy.

Suddenly an explosive, shattering roar came from below. Behind the flash of gunfire, Ontaquos glimpsed the face of the younger brother. Ontaquos heard the grunt of surprise as a bullet struck Metacom. Then he heard a splash as the body crumpled and sprawled in the soggy swamp. Metacom lay silent.

Ontaquos groaned. Tears ran down his cheeks. He pulled his knife blade from his belt and slashed his arm. With blood running from his fingertips, he tapped his mother's shoulder and motioned the others to follow. Each one slid silently through the darkness and blended into the forest.

XLI
GOOD BYE NETOP

Caleb sat waiting. It was dark. Shadows flickered in the moonlight. It seemed he'd been there for hours. Then in the distance he heard gunfire and shouting. An hour after the gunfire ceased, he stood on the path with his gun raised at the sound of running feet. "Halt." He aimed his flintlock.

"Don't shoot." It was one of the Swanzey men. He slapped Caleb on the back. "We got him! He be dead! King Philip and several of his Council. I be heading home to tell the town." He hurried down the path.

Caleb challenged more figures and recognized more of his own platoon. "What happened?"

"The Plimoth troops attacked the Wampanoags first. "Twas a complete surprise. Most of the heathens were captured or killed. Philip was shot by the Heathen guide. A few escaped along the bay path, but they can't get too far. The Plimoth troops under Captain Church are in pursuit.

"I've posted a few of our men back on the trail. Ye'll be the last sentry. If ye see or hear anything, fire yer gun and the others will come to yer aid. I think the Wampanoags be all gone, but ye stay here 'til daybreak." He clapped Caleb on the shoulder. "The war be over!"

Caleb grinned. It was hard to believe. He watched the sergeant disappear into the night gloom and sat back in the shadows. It was very quiet and nearly dawn. He strained his eyes in the darkness and listened intently for any sound.

A large raccoon ambled along the path. Caleb sat motionless and stared silently at the creature. It stood up, sniffing the air. It looked at Caleb, then waddled off in the underbrush toward the spring not far from the path.

Caleb sat rubbing his pendant. The first slivers of dawn's light, stretching across the horizon, changed night blackness into a misty grey. He was about to get up when a slight movement caught his eye. He hadn't heard a sound, but he was sure he'd seen something move. He held his breath.

In the lightening shadows of early dawn, he saw one form and then another glide silently along a tiny path that led to the main one where he sat hidden. He waited until they were opposite his hiding place, then leapt onto the path, gun ready, and shouted, "Halt!"

The figures froze. He heard a woman's startled muffled cry. A child's voice wavered in fear. All the figures stood very still. Caleb held his gun ready to shoot. He saw one woman bend to pick up a frightened child. A tall figure stood protectively between him and the silent group. He aimed his gun at this one's chest.

Caleb approached cautiously. At that moment, the first rays of the orange sunrise burst across the bay and reflected on his copper pendant shimmering in the brightness.

He was about to discharge his gun to alert the others, when he heard the tall Indian suck in a deep breath and murmur, "Netop?"

Caleb peered intently into the painted face. How worn and thin his friend looked. "Netop," he replied.

Neither one moved. Then Caleb smiled
and slowly lowered his gun and rested it
against a tree. Ontaquos smiled as he stood
silently watching. They eyed each other.
Finally Caleb motioned his friend to move
on. He turned his back on the group.

Ontaquos motioned his people to wait
and turned toward his mother. She nodded
sadly and handed him the child. The child
clung to Ontaquos as he approached Caleb.
Soothing her with gentle Indian words, he
calmed her, patting and rocking her in his
arms.

Caleb's eyes opened wide in surprise when
the deerskin wrapping fell away and he saw
the child's blonde, curly hair framing the
blue-eyed youngster's face. The youngster
stared into his clear blue eyes with a curious
look of recognition. She reached toward
him.

Caleb took the child and cuddled her.
She poked a finger at his eye and grabbed a
handful of his hair. Ontaquos pointed to her
and said, "Manchaug."

Caleb looked perplexed. Ontaquos
shrugged his shoulders. The little girl tugged
at the copper pendant. Caleb held her in one

arm and with his free hand, slipped the cord over his head. He handed the pendant to Ontaquos, who reached out and took it. He held it in the palm of his hand, then looked at Caleb. Their eyes spoke. He slipped the loop over his head and fingered his pendant.

"Good-bye, Netop," Caleb said.

"Good-bye Netop," answered Ontaquos. He squeezed Caleb's shoulder.

Once again Caleb turned his back on the group, retrieved his gun, and, cradling the little girl, walked slowly along the path to Swanzey. He turned back in the morning sunlight and saw Ontaquos standing at a bend in the path, waiting for his people to slip out of sight into the forest.

Caleb waved.

Ontaquos' arm flashed a final farewell.

Several hours later, just before he reached home, Caleb heard a sound far to the North. He stopped to listen. Crows signalled the presence of intruders in a cacophony of disapproval. Above the faint sounds, Caleb heard the cry of a lone wolf echoing against the northern hills.

GLOSSARY

Ottucke	Deer
Niccone	Black Crow
Whauksus	Red Fox
Netop	Friend
Kuttiomp	A great Buck
Nunummatin	North Wind
Shannuke	Squirrel
Pequawas	Grey Fox
Awuanaguss	Englishman
Chauquaqock	Sword-men
Wampanoag	Eastern People
Hobomok	Spirit of the night
Ontaquos	Wolf
Tomaquog	Beaver
Wawunnes	A Buck
Mauntop	Mount Hope
Succotash	Corn and bean soup

TO ORDER
"TWO PATHS IN THE WILDERNESS"

Please send ----- copies @ $9.50 each (20% discount
for orders 25 and over) plus handling and shipping to:

Name---

Address---

State---------Zip code--------------------------

And mail to:

> Ellen E. Wilson
> 5459 Florence Point
> Fernandina, FL 32034